I0588532

NEVER SAY DIE

published by
The Canberra Speculative Fiction Guild

Never Say Die

To the best of the publisher and editors' knowledge, no artificial intelligence, large language model, generative pre-trained transformer, or other non-human generative tools were used in the creation of works within this book.

For full credits of contributors for this publication, see the credits at the back of this book.

Cover illustration by Madison Lee.
Skull illustration sourced from Vecteezy.com.

ISBN: 978-0-6484146-8-1 (Paperback), 978-0-6484146-9-8 (E-book)

The authors and contributors acknowledge the traditional owners of the many lands on which the stories in this book were written and edited. The Canberra Speculative Fiction Guild acknowledges the Ngunnawal and Ngambri people as the traditional owners of the Canberra region. We pay our respects to their Elders, past and present.

Published by CSFG Publishing
PO Box 1150
Dickson ACT 2602
Australia

To the ones lost
and the ones who lost them

More from the CSFG

CONTENTS

FOREWORD

Death destroys a man; the idea of death saves him.
—E.M. Forster, *Howards End* (1910)

THERE ARE FEW things in existence that draw as much fear, and as much intrigue, as death. Throughout human history there has been an endless drive to understand it, to explore the themes and experiences around it. Fiction lets us hold ideas in the palms of our hands, even ones as huge and as terrifying as death; to see and examine and become familiar without the pain and threat of reality. When we first heard the concept for this year's anthology, myself and the committee knew it was going to make the perfect addition to our roster of works.

I have an interesting relationship with death. It visited me early in life, and with the kind of suddenness and tragedy that makes you wish it had just been a story. In the years since, it has felt like death was there with me, not as an abstract but a constant inevitability. A part of life, not the end of it. It seems fitting that once again death has visited me here, in the first anthology I have had the privilege of participating in.

Ironically, for an anthology titled *Never Say Die*, this collection worked very hard to do exactly that. From the multiple transfers of hands to the seemingly endless stream of setbacks both within the book and outside it in the lives of us its caretakers, this was not a publication that came into the world easily.

And yet, here it is. A collection of the words from some established, some new, all amazing writers. Death is examined closely, intimately, mechanically, and spiritually in the stories and poems they provided. All of these pieces hold something exciting and new, but they also speak to the constant uncertainty and exploration of death by humans throughout our history.

This anthology wouldn't have been possible without the help of a large collection of people willing to step up and share the load when things really were do or die. I would like to thank my fellow members of the CSFG committee; C.Z. Tacks, Americo Alvarenga, Lee Cope, Addie Ellicott, Richard Niven, Trevor Fritzlaff, and Victor Yii for throwing their support behind this collection when the editor had to step back. I want to thank our first readers, our proof readers, our editors, our typesetters, and our promoters for all the hard work they contributed. There were so many folks who were happy to help out and pitch in, and you can see all of their names on the credit page. Without them, this book truly wouldn't have been possible.

I also want to thank all of the writers whose work appears in this book. Patience in uncertainty is always an important skill when you are submitting works, but the constant delays in getting this thing moving tested that. I thank all of them for their patience and grace while we figured it all out, and for their professionalism through the editing phase. Every one of them was a delight to work with. I also should thank them for their stories, of course. Without those, this book would be significantly more boring.

Another thank you as well to all the writers who submitted, but whose works do not appear in this anthology. Writing is an intimate exercise in self examination, and to share what you have written is an act that feels vulnerable and raw. You were brave for doing so, and the future is bright. Keep writing, because now more than ever the world needs that kind of creativity, and only you can make that.

I hope you enjoy this death defying collection. Like death feels like an ending, but is really just a beginning of something unknowable, so too the ending of this foreword is the beginning of something fantastic.

Fionn MacPherson.

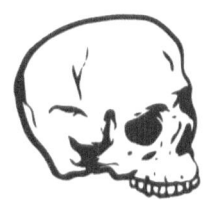

NEVER SAID

Monica Carroll

The bucket hat slid back   falling down behind my chair   so
my head got dragged back so   it fell too   so
it dropped onto the rug   so
    I felt surprised and itchy   so
    my head smouldered   on the rug   so
    house flies winged out of gums   out from my gums   so
a plum blowie clung to my eyeball my wet eyeball   so
house flies streamed   from my gums   so
a man thumped through   the corridors   in my head   so
    his boots fell heavy   thunderous   so
    he stomped through   the corridors in my head   so
he pushed himself from   my mouth   so
shoved a microphone to my lips   so
he stomped from my mouth   of my mouth so
    my mouth and all the flies began talking   so
    he reported   the talking we made   so
    my mouth and all the flies talking   so
my words have no sound   so   he records me   so
he and the flies   write down my words so
my words have no sound   so   he records me   so
    my words have no sound so   he records me   so
so

1

Monica Carroll is a researcher, horror writer, and book artist. Her forthcoming series on Fear & How to Write Horror will be published by Dark Cave Press in 2025. Carroll's fiction and poetry has been anthologised and published widely, including in the *Anthology of Australian Prose Poetry* (Melbourne University Press, 2020) and *Westerly Humanities Review* (University of Utah, 2018). Her collaborative non-fiction works include *The Knowing of Artists' Books* (University of Iowa Press, 2023) and *Everyday Words. Ten Australian Poets* (Puncher and Wattman, 2019). Sign up to be notified of her upcoming works at www.monicacarroll.com.au.

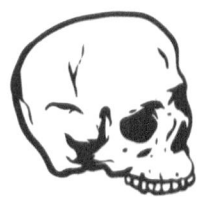

A Shortcut via the New Tunnel, M-ate

C.H. Pearce

W E'LL TAKE THE new tunnel, m-ate," says Reddy from the driver's seat, his inside voice reverberating in the car, and making me squeeze my eyes shut.

The traffic's heavy crawling out of Sydney. I crack open an eye and watch him sidelong from the passenger seat, wary.

Reddy uses 'mate' for colleagues he doesn't like. He always calls me Liam, or 'the intern,' except for the times he gets mixed-up after a few drinks and calls me his son's name, then denies it. Am I in his bad books?

There's the freeway to the left, the one we always take on the five-and-a-half-hour road trip home to Wagga Wagga. Tank's three-quarters full. GPS is on the dash. Neither of us know Sydney well. I had another surgery yesterday to repair the last surgical repair. I'm woozy, sore, and yeah, tetchy. I look like a gutted fish under my layers.

The nurse told me not to travel. I lied to Reddy. Don't want us both to miss work on Monday, and draw attention.

Reddy veers right.

"What new tunnel?" I ask.

"The new tunnel. M-ate."

"Why are you pronouncing it like that?" I fail to keep the irritation from my voice. I get pissy after surgery.

Reddy's been an engineer for like, forty years. Sixty-something, divorced, with a son my age who won't see him. I'm the only colleague who will listen to his rant-loop, at work and at the pub, about how everything's his ex-wife's fault. Reading between the lines, it's mostly Reddy's fault, but I nod and make my face sympathetic. I'm not *that* stupid.

I tried not to become friends; he's my supervisor while I'm on my uni internship, and I'm no suck-up. Yet, he's driving me home from "medical tourism" in Sydney in his Toyota Camry—again—so guess how well that went. My parents don't know about my health issues. I love them, but if you'd met them, you'd understand. I'm supposed to be doing an engineering degree. I'm supposed to be the promising kid.

We leave the traffic behind. Must be a fat toll ahead. I don't say anything—it's too late to turn around, and Reddy will get pissed off.

There is the wide mouth of the tunnel ahead, getting closer. A Variable Message Sign overhangs the darkness.

The M8. I misheard.

Inside the tunnel, it's muffled except for the thrum of the car, like I'm wearing headphones. Darkness, then sickly light. The e-tag doesn't beep.

The GPS loses reception. It lags, searching.

Reddy drums the wheel. "Tunnel's more expensive, but it'll shave twenty minutes off our trip. No one else is using it. Suckers."

We're the suckers. Only tourists like us would pay the toll. I try to google how much it costs, but there's no reception.

The trip to Wagga should take five-and-a-half hours. The GPS said so when we left the hospital. I'd shuffled to the car in a daze, even though they said not to get out of bed so soon, supported by Reddy like I was drunk. I'd looked at the dash, the GPS's estimate: five hours, twenty-eight minutes. Saving twenty minutes is a drop in the ocean, but Reddy's all about efficient routes; at least he'll get a kick out of it.

We whip past identikit sections of tunnel, pale yellow-green, new asphalt underneath the wheels. More Variable Message Signs flash by overhead. Digital ads glow from the walls. This one is a smiling woman advertising affordable family lawyers. She's a toothy, middle-aged lady in a suit, her blonde hair pulled back so tight in a bun it tugs at the skin of her temples.

"You look . . ." Reddy glances at me sidelong. "Sure you're right to travel today, Aidan?"

I don't trust myself to lie without puking. Nor can I summon the energy to remind him my name's Liam, and have an argument about whether or not I misheard. I roll down the window. We've seen each other puke on nights out. I'd prefer not to repeat that at the start of a five-and-a-half hour road trip in a friend's car. Neither of us should drink like we do. We're both on meds—I've got my stuff, Reddy has a heart thing. Since we have the same vice, we can hardly judge one another.

The Variable Message Sign overhead reads CLOSE WINDOWS, RECIRCULATE AIR.

I roll up the window. Press the recirculate button on the air con.

We pass an advertisement for my uni, directly followed by another for a different uni, which feels passive-aggressive. There are laughing students my age in both, as well as the older blonde lady.

It's the same woman in every ad. Only the cohort of students are different. I'm bad with faces, but not *that* bad. She must be doing well for herself. If she's a celebrity, I don't know her.

We're clocking 120, and the woman's smiles stretch thin.

"Long fucken tunnel," observes Reddy conversationally. "Radio?"

I flick through stations. It crackles. We almost get a voice.

We drive for twenty minutes.

—

Forty-five minutes.

I remember the machines in the hospital when I woke up, the bloody beeping noises escalating to a discordant chorus. Reddy was sitting at my bedside. I'd hazily asked what all that fucken noise was, moved stupidly to rip out the breathing tube and the cannula, wanting nothing more than to go back to sleep, only it was too loud. His saggy face contorted like he was either worried, or had heartburn—I have trouble reading his face sometimes. Sweat on his forehead, hand clutching his chest, the other one on mine. He had leant forward and said seriously: "That's the machine that goes 'bing,' Aidan." Reddy can be funny under pressure, when he's not being a dick.

Despite being unsettled, I'm enjoying the quiet now.

Reddy is sweating bullets again, gritting his teeth. He won't admit anything's bothering him. Like he wouldn't admit anything was wrong in thirty years of marriage until *after* it exploded.

I'm waiting for him to say it. I know *he* wants *me* to, so he can be annoyed with me.

I won't crack.

Reddy's speeding. The ladies' smiles look like white contrails. This one is laughing, a family pack from Red Rooster plated up like a home-cooked meal at the dinner table, with the box prominently displayed. There's another laughing middle-aged woman hand-feeding her a chip, and a skinny guy my age who's presumably play-acting her kid or a colleague. A real family, or a work family? The guy looks like me. It's gone before I can double-take—he's not me, obviously.

Why are all the ads slight variants of the same thing? Why are they all this blonde, toothy, ecstatically happy woman? The same lazy advertising company, maybe?

"Long fucken tunnel," I say, swallowing bile.

To my surprise, Reddy explodes into laughter. "This'll take us halfway to Wagga."

I'm not worried.

I'm not worried, in particular, about getting stuck.

There are cameras. Somebody will come get you.

—

We have half a tank.

"Turn around," I blurt. "Backtrack while we have enough fuel."

Reddy gestures with one hand, almost smacking me in the face. "It's a one-way fucken tunnel, Liam."

"There are no other cars. Turn back."

"You're off your tits on your pain meds. Stupid idea." Reddy sets his jaw.

He's used to having authority. Feels obligated to act like he knows what's going on.

It's fine at work. You make grumps like Reddy feel they're in charge, then quietly do your own thing. Here . . .

I can't wrestle Reddy for the steering wheel. He's twice my weight even if I *weren't* worried about busting my stitches.

I try a different tack. "The blonde woman in the ads. You recognise her?"

"Nope." Reddy's dismissal is sharp as a slap.

He clears his throat. More gently, assures me: "Any minute, we'll come out the other side, and you'll feel silly."

—

I popped more pain meds. I'm too relaxed for what's going on. I'm lightheaded, my bandages sticking to the blood oozing from my wound. The air con's off.

"Almost out of petrol." It's been five hours, twenty-eight minutes.

"Think I don't fucken know . . ." Reddy goes off, shouting. I let his rant wash over me. Now he's started, he's like a wind-up toy; best to let it run its course. Reddy gets like this to blow off steam, but it's never personal. That is, it's never personal towards *me*—it's often pretty personal about his family, and colleagues he doesn't like, including management and every 'muppet' subcontractor on the project.

We drive till the car sputters to a stop.

Reddy pulls his hands over his face.

He won't admit he doesn't know what's happening. That he can't fix it.

I won't, either. What good would it do to panic? That's what they say, when you get lost in the bush, or the desert. Don't panic. Can't remember what else they say. Stay put?

I put a hand to his shoulder and pat it several times, hesitantly, like I'm touching a dead fish. He doesn't throw me off, or acknowledge it.

—

"I'll walk and get help," says Reddy.

It's stifling in the car, filled with the stench of recirculated bad breath and festering sores.

He's pushing open the driver's side door.

My phone's nearly out of battery. No reception.

I'm sweating buckets, clutching my abdomen, failing to unclip my own seatbelt without hissing in pain. "I'll go with you."

I don't want to be alone.

Reddy's face is haggard, his eyes sincere. "Keep the water. Don't move. Won't be long," he promises. Like he has control over anything, ever.

It's difficult to talk. I concentrate on breathing. I should have gotten antibiotics to-go, along with the opiates.

I grasp for words to make him not walk down the tunnel. If I can find the right combination, I can convince him.

"Do you reckon we, like, maybe . . ." *Nice argument, loser. Really convincing. Go on. Rip it off like a band-aid.* "Do you remember in the hospital, when all those bloody machines were beeping and the nurses were racing around, and I wanted to sleep, and you were clutching your chest like you were having a heart attack and making a stupid joke?"

"Yeah, no," lies Reddy, badly.

I barrel on, throwing more words out. "What if this is it, at the end of everything—just big fat fucken nothing? Look, sorry, but I'd at least rather not be here *alone*. Parting ways feels like the stupidest, most pointless thing we could do at this point. Even if we're *not* dead—let's take a sec, examine all the possibilities, Reddy—if we are not dead, then we are lost, and when you get lost, you're supposed to stay put—"

He reaches over the centre console, and ruffles my sweaty hair.

Does he get me?

Reddy says: "That's for when you get lost in the bush or the desert. There are only two directions here, backwards and forwards. There has got to be an escape door."

"—so why haven't we fucken seen one—"

"I've been an engineer for forty bloody years, I reckon I can figure this tunnel out. But you, Aidan—you're off your tits, you have a fever, and you fucken lied to me about being cleared to travel today."

He climbs out of the car, leaving the windows down, the doors ajar.

Through the windshield, I watch him walk into the tunnel's humming throat.

C.H. Pearce is an artist and an Aurealis and Brave New Weird Award-nominated and Ditmar Award-winning writer of horror-tinged speculative fiction. She has a background in history and archives, lives in Canberra with her family, and her hobbies include fan art, for which she's won Ditmar Awards. Her short fiction has been published in *Body of Work* anthology, *Cosmic Horror Monthly*, *The Off-Season: An Anthology of Coastal New Weird*, and more. Find her work and links to her print shop and social media on chpearce.net.

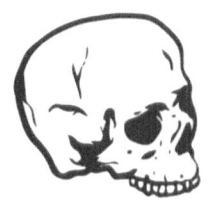

THE STORM

Trevor Fritzaff

B ENITA DIDN'T MIND that chill pricked at her ears and cold sea breeze slid inside her sleeves. She hugged her thermos and pushed on, up the meandering path to the little bench overlooking the beach.

It had been their ritual, hers and Satoshi's, since their retirement. Twice each week, so long as they were feeling up to it.

In winter she rugged herself up. Long pink puffer jacket, footy beanie on her head and two pairs of socks in her boots. She sat there with her thermos of coffee and faced the elements. It was poignant, but still comforting, especially when a storm came whipping across the choppy waters. He had loved the storms.

—

One Tuesday morning, another old woman sat down at the far end of the bench.

Benita wasn't happy about that. It wasn't getting any easier, struggling up that hill, and she couldn't help feeling resentful of anybody who disturbed her tranquillity at the place where she felt so close to Satoshi.

She had seen the woman approach and silently willed her to keep walking past, but she sat down anyway and gave a friendly "hello". A grey-haired lady. Thick black coat and matching little hat. Walking stick.

Benita returned the greeting, added a polite nod, then shifted her attention back to the storm she was watching.

Still a long way off, she thought, although they could arrive sooner than expected. Its veil was gently smudging out the hills on the far side of the bay.

The clouds, the cold air and the warming coffee, they always put Benita at peace with herself, and with Satoshi. Now this woman had broken the spell.

"I'm Thea," said the walking-stick woman, her voice inflecting upwards as if she was only just realising the fact.

Benita looked her up and down. She could be a "talker".

"Oh," the walking stick woman shook her head, "No, I don't intend to blather on at you about trivialities." She swivelled herself around in Benita's direction. "But I do have some information for you that I think you'll find rather interesting."

Definitely a talker, then, and with indications of religiosity as well. The worst sort. "Mmm," was all Benita said, annoyed at the prospect of having to walk back down the hill again so soon.

"Yes," the woman turned away, resting her hands on the walking stick and nodding slowly to herself, "because I know a bit about you and Satoshi." She glanced across at Benita with a smile. "Very special people."

A tiny rush of cold air into Benita's mouth. She stared hard, but there was nothing familiar in the woman's face.

"I mean to say, Cambridge, CERN, and so many citations of your papers. You were quite a pair, weren't you?"

It occurred to Benita that she hadn't called the woman a "talker" out loud.

"Who are you?"

Thea's smile widened.

"I'm just somebody who is interested in having a little chat with you about the old days. The double slit experiment, perhaps?"

Benita left the silence alone while she considered the woman. Her eyes wandered from walking stick to hat and back again, searching for recognition. *Suspicious odds*, she thought. *Two little old ladies, both into quantum physics, on one park bench.*

"I don't, umm—"

"Come on, Benita. You know that nobody ever truly manages to reconcile that experiment with their imagination. And you, you have a wonderful imagination. You will have considered the issues as deeply as anybody I can think of."

Thea sat back and gestured with her walking stick, as if she was relaxing into an old story.

"You take a tiny particle . . . of anything, really—but a photon or an electron are the classics—and send it through a tiny slit. It hits a detector on the other side. Very simple. But then, you—"

"I'm familiar with the experiment. I've performed versions of it myself and lectured about its implic—"

"Just let an old woman finish her story, Benita. I enjoy this bit, all right?"

Benita stopped and shrugged. *Get on with it then*, she thought, and took another swig of her coffee.

"So," Thea continued, "then you put a second slit next to the first one, and give the little particle a choice. Does it go through the left slit, or the right?"

She stopped abruptly and tilted her head, watching Benita with the hint of a smile.

"Oh." Benita sat up straight and put her coffee down on the bench. "Are you giving me the punch-line?"

Thea nodded happily.

Benita leaned over for a conspiratorial whisper.

"Well, effectively, it can go through . . . both."

"Isn't that cool? It's so cool," Thea beamed. Then she furrowed her brow and murmured, "But, Benita, how can one little particle go through two different places at once? How does it even know that the second slit is there?"

Benita grinned, recalling the lesson it had taken so many years to grasp.

"It's as Mr. Bohr said, isn't it? If quantum mechanics hasn't profoundly shocked you, then you haven't understood it yet."

"But *you* understood it, didn't you, Benita? You and Satoshi."

Quiet descended. There was damp in Benita's eyes.

"I *wish*," she said, looking into the distance. "But nobody ever understands it. Not really."

Thea's voice sounded ethereal.

"I don't mean to distress you, Benita, but I know how many questions you raised, how many equations you re-derived, how many long-held beliefs you stress-tested. And yet it's still not quite satisfying, is it?

That's why I thought I'd run something past you."

Benita blinked the damp into a tiny sparkle, roused by the prospect of a discussion more challenging than an old widow had become resigned to.

"So, Benita, a tiny particle is capable of being in, or at least aware of, two places, or more, at once. So it seems. Although I use the word *aware* with caution. It's the best your language can do, I'm afraid."

Benita took a breath. "Well, perhaps the particle isn't really *in* any one place or moving in any particular way until it encounters that detector. Maybe it's the interaction itself which causes the particle to *be* in a specific spot. But it is certainly a challenge to get one's head around all that."

Thea nodded. "More than a challenge, I would say, for any being whose life depends upon following things as they move around the place. Your quantum mechanics asks you to accept that a thing can be in one place, and then be somewhere else, without ever having *been* anywhere between the two?"

"It does," she said with a sly smile. "I'm not an expert in these things, but I am also aware of what you call 'entangled particles'. I think that's where one particle *knows*—sorry, I realise that word is clumsy—but it knows *instantaneously*, no matter how far away they are separated, when the other particle has had an interaction."

"There are circumstances where some properties of particles can be nonlocal. You're getting into some rather tricky areas, Thea."

Thea raised the walking stick again. "At some level. At some fundamental level. Would you agree that there could be a sort of . . . connectedness . . . of everything . . . all the time?"

Benita kept smiling. "Goodness me. Jumping right into the long grass, aren't you? Well, perhaps that could be the case, possibly. But your so-called *connectedness* is a rather difficult concept to *connect* with."

"Exactly so. And goodness knows, you've tried, haven't you?"

Benita closed her eyes for a wistful little sigh. "Yes, we certainly tried." Then she added, "But you know, Thea, I still don't think that any of us understand what an electron even *is*. Let alone the connectedness of everything. Mmm." Her forefinger signalled a memory. "That brings to mind another one of Mr. Bohr's supposed quotes: 'Tomorrow will be wonderful, because tonight I don't understand anything.' Satoshi and I, we put in a lot of effort trying to reach that 'tomorrow'."

They both sat back and rested their attention on the storm for a while. The wind was rising, blustering around and bringing occasional spikes of icy air. Rain was visible over the water and the hills across the bay had disappeared. Thea turned back to Benita.

"That breeze has certainly got a kick in it. Would you mind? Pouring a little of your coffee into that thermos lid for me?"

Benita poured the coffee, placed the thermos back on the bench, and their arms stretched out as Benita passed the lid across.

"Thank you." Thea took a slow sip. "That's much better." She leaned her walking stick against the bench and cupped what was left of the warm coffee in both hands.

"Are you a Brian Ferry fan, Benita?"

Benita recoiled slightly. "Goodness. That takes me back. Was he into physics too?"

"Not sure, really. Never met him. But in exchange for your quotes by Mr. Bohr, I have one of his song titles for you. Bit of a banger, actually." She paused, and her eyes lingered on Benita's face. "This isn't something I usually do, you know, but I came here today to show you where you and Satoshi were heading, while you're still old enough to appreciate it. Satoshi did. So," and she allowed herself a tiny chuckle, "as Mr. Ferry might say, '*This is Tomorrow*', Benita."

Benita's hand eased around the thermos and took it back onto her lap.

"Look, I don't want to be unfriendly, but who are you? And what are you going on about?"

"Now we're getting to it." Thea's eyes locked on with intent, "I'm afraid I'm talking about the general gobsmackingness of reality."

Benita forced herself to smile politely. "That's nice." She pointed to Thea's hand. "I'm going to need my lid back."

"You are still deeply troubled by not understanding the true nature of existence, Benita. And I believe that you have earned a brief, but very special reward before you go."

Benita paused at that, but did her best to keep the smile on. "Where am I going, then?"

Thea's stare turned sympathetic, and somehow more unnerving.

"You're going . . . to have to forget about your sense of *self*. That's where you're going." She waved her free hand up and down between Benita's boots and beanie. "We both know that, miraculous as you are, you're still just a template for a temporary arrangement of immortal particles that entropy has been scratching away at for over eighty years.

15

Sooner or later they'll have to do away with all of this 'Benita' business. And that's a wrench, isn't it? Very tough for any human. Bit of a disappointment, in fact.

"But I am going to show you something deeper. Something about how you will go on beyond . . . well, no. *You* won't, but . . . oh, God, it's so difficult to avoid this human-consciousness point of view, isn't it? So limited. And gets in your way all the time."

Thea took another sip and passed back the empty thermos lid. She planted her walking stick in front of her legs and stood up with a creaky sigh.

"Let's cut to the chase, as they say. Want a backstage pass to the whole 'connectedness of everything' show? Just for a second or two? That's all you'll be able to take, I'm afraid. But it will be a brief glimpse of something that completely eludes the human consciousness.

"Of course, as Benita, you're not within a million years of comprehending this, so I'll have to plug you into some evolutionary enhancements as a bonus. Should be quite a buzz. You ready?"

Benita had done her best to be polite. She closed her eyes for a moment, adjusted her puffer jacket, and deliberately looked past Thea and out towards her storm.

It had come unexpectedly close and the clouds were darkening.

"No doubt you just want this wacky old bat with the walking stick to take the hint, toddle off, and leave you alone to your reminiscences."

Benita nodded gently, but her eyes were wide at the occasional spots of rain already appearing on the asphalt in front of her.

She could feel Thea's eyes drilling into the top of her beanie. The voice was deathly quiet.

"I haven't come all this way to leave you with nothing more than reminiscences, Benita . . . Please? As moments go, this is the biggie. I guarantee it."

Benita shook her head defiantly as she stared at the waves crashing onto a now-deserted foreshore. It looked as though this storm was one she wouldn't manage to avoid.

She gripped her thermos tight and lifted the lid from her lap to screw it back on. That was when she relented and looked up again at Thea.

When their eyes met they exchanged a brief glint of what Benita might have inadequately referred to as mutual understanding . . . if she was able to speak. Then the walking-stick woman smiled and wandered away down the path.

The storm arrived with swirling winds that lifted scraps of paper high into the air. Lashing rain bent the heaviest branches on the fat old date palms and sent the thermos lid flying into the grass. The leftover coffee dribbled out of the thermos itself, as it slowly slipped from Benita's fingers, and rolled along the seat.

Trevor Fritzlaff is a member of the CSFG novel and short story groups. The first three thousand words of his novel *It's just some old book* won the 2024 Marlowe and Christie Novel Prize in the UK for unpublished authors. This is his first time in print. He and Jenny live in Canberra, have two grown up kids, and are part-time doggie sitters for Mabel and Rosie.

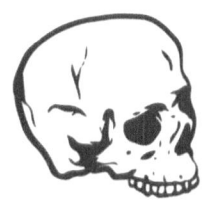

Downloaded

Michael T. Schaper

S ERENA FELT A little strange as she stepped out of the clinic, the dog following behind her. It was a lovely warm day, with just a wisp of wind. Everything felt different.

Not surprising, since she'd just made herself immortal.

What a gift! She felt elated and energised as she thought of the opportunities that the procedure had just opened up to her. Time enough now to do everything and anything, to be anyone she might think of. The possibilities were endless. It was as if the days before this one were just a vague dream, a life totally different from the world she was now entering.

She made her way up the side alley the clinic was hidden within. Serena paused as she reached the main street just a few metres further along, stopping to check the road before going any further. It was full of people just doing what ordinary human beings did any normal day. Shopping. Talking on their phones. Getting on and off buses. Parking cars. Meandering down the sidewalk. She tried to see if she could recognise a few of them, but then she'd never been good with faces.

No one had noticed her coming out of the shadows, as far as she could tell. She slipped out into the crowd, the dog trotting alongside her, and hoped that she just looked like an ordinary member of the public.

She was fundamentally different to them, now. One day they'd be dead, and she wouldn't. That would certainly make anyone feel special, she thought.

Her head was spinning, but the nurses had assured her that this was perfectly normal. Serena had spent almost the whole morning attached to various electrodes, EEG monitors, wires and the like. She'd been anaesthetised at one stage, and there had been numerous probes inserted through her ears and nose at various points of the procedure.

Her nose was still irritated. She found herself sneezing once, twice, then a third time. A headache was surely on its way.

Her time in the clinic had passed excruciatingly slowly. It had taken a long while to download her entire consciousness, but it would be worth it, as long as she wasn't caught.

The procedure was highly experimental, and so many volunteers had died during the testing phase that regulators were unwilling to authorise it.

All of this was on the sly, banned on both ethical and practical grounds. Receiving this treatment meant entering a prohibited zone where you didn't ask or say too much if you wanted to be on the program. Places were bought and sold on the black market, and the cost was astronomical. Those caught undertaking it, both giving and receiving, were almost always prosecuted. Not surprisingly, the clinic had been keen to get her away out the door as soon as they'd finished with her.

"*Be careful*," they'd advised, "*and for heaven's sake, don't say a word to anyone else.*"

Little wonder that she'd felt so uptight during the process, and that the anxiety was still with her.

She heard a sharp yap, and looked down at the small white terrier at her feet. The little dog was looking keenly into the street, tail wagging, as if it had seen someone it recognised.

What was she doing with the animal? She wasn't really a dog person, but the clinic staff had insisted she take it, saying only that someone would be around to collect it from her in due course.

Serena noticed a movement out of the edge of her vision, and tensed up. It was just a woman, walking past her. For a moment Serena thought she looked familiar. Had she been looking at Serena? Was she being followed?

Relax, she told herself. Don't jump at shadows. Try to be calm, and don't rush. You've literally got all the time in the world now.

Serena settled down at the next café she came across, finding an outside table to accommodate the dog. Best to act normal, she thought as she waited to place her order. Try to act as if she'd been doing nothing particularly special or different today.

She thought about what had just been done to her, the amazing reality of the procedure. The clinic staff had set in train the continuation of her own personality, all downloaded and stored electronically. When she passed away, this could be combined with samples of her DNA the clinic had also taken, downloaded into a clone and—voila!—she'd be back. Or at least as close as possible.

As her mind followed the steps of the procedure—the upload, the cloning, the download—she remembered one of the multiple failsafes she had been told were a part of the process. The data. Her spare copy of the data. Where was it? She felt a chill of fear spike through her.

The clinic had promised that they'd upload it all into the cloud and give her a backup copy, but she didn't seem to have it on her. In her daze, she hadn't even thought to enquire about it when she left, although she knew that the backup was critical. If something went wrong, this would all have been for nothing.

She was halfway to her feet, ready to return to the clinic, when a voice jolted her back to reality.

"Hello?" A figure loomed up out of nowhere and faced her across the table. A stranger, and it was definitely not the waiter.

Serena realised with a start that it was the same woman who'd passed her just a few minutes ago. Again, Serena felt that sense of familiarity. Was this someone she had met before?

The dog yapped and wagged his tail, regarding their visitor with interest. Serena didn't know much about dogs. Did that mean the beast was happy or worried?

Without another word the stranger sat down. She summoned the waiter, ordering two cafés au lait without waiting for Serena to state what she wanted.

"One for each of us," she said. "I'm sure it's still your favourite. And the caffeine might help with your headache."

How did she know that? Serena's heart rate jumped. Had this woman been watching her come out of the clinic? Who was she?

The waiter returned with their coffees, placing them on the table between them. He gave the two of them a strange look, and seemed on the verge of saying something before thinking better of it and instead heading back inside the café.

"Perhaps you might like a pinch of sugar?" Without asking, the woman scooped out a teaspoonful, tipped it into Serena's cup, and stirred. "There you go. Might make you feel better."

Serena watched, taken aback. She wasn't used to people being so presumptuous. She didn't actually like sugar, but this woman was acting so strange it seemed too minor a matter to raise.

They sat there in the midday sun, silently, awkwardly. The woman watched Serena intently as she drank her coffee, then nodded happily. Serena remained frozen to her chair, petrified as to what might happen next. Was this woman an undercover police officer? If she'd been staking out the clinic, Serena could be under arrest any moment.

She cursed her luck. All that angst and effort, and here she'd been caught. She hadn't even walked out with her download. She could feel the headache continuing to pound away.

"Are you following me?" she finally summoned up the courage to ask.

The stranger looked her over once more, and smiled. "Of course I am," she said, "it's important that I do so."

"It is?"

"Well, yes, given how much I paid for this."

A curious turn of phrase. Serena studied the woman opposite her one more time. Tall, black hair, slightly stocky. Not that dissimilar to herself. Perhaps in different circumstances they could have been friends.

Then Serena realised the face she was looking at was not just familiar.

It was her own.

She blinked once, twice, trying to be certain that her vision hadn't suddenly gone awry. Was this even possible? Suddenly her world felt turned upside down, surreal. Surely this couldn't be right.

The stranger remained at ease, as if nothing unusual was going on.

Serena considered the situation and tried to weigh up the facts. If the other woman had her face, and her build, they had to be clones. There wasn't any other explanation. And if that was the case, it meant one of two possibilities.

"Are . . . you my backup?" Serena asked quietly, hopefully.

The woman just smiled back at her, a sad pitying look, and shook her head. "No, I think you've rather missed the point. The clinic didn't tell you?"

"Tell me what?"

"Really, they should have explained all this, but I believe they were a bit rushed this morning. At least, that's what they told me when I came in."

A cold realisation struck Serena. A horror.

"If you're not the clone, then . . . am I the backup?"

"No, you're not a backup," the stranger said, patting the dog affectionately. The terrier's tail wagged back and forth happily, contentment on its face.

Serena let out the breath she was holding. Well, that was a relief.

Then the stranger continued. "Well, you're not really the true backup, is what I meant to say."

"Sorry?"

"You're not a backup, just the test copy," the woman said. "The clinic always conducts a test run before the real backup is downloaded, of course. Just common sense. Makes sure everything's right before we get serious. And it leaves us with a decoy, in case we have a run-in with the law. So you're not the real thing, neither human nor backup." She winced. "Sorry about that. I realise it must be a bit of a shock."

Serena sipped the last of her coffee, screwing her nose up at the sweet taste of the sugar, and tried to gather herself. Well, she assumed they were her own thoughts, and not something that belonged to someone else. *Am I not a real person?* she wondered. *What am I? Whose thoughts, whose emotions, am I feeling right now? Is anything . . . well . . . really me?* Suddenly existence itself seemed something that belonged to strangers, not herself.

"So what happens now?" she asked.

"I'm off," the stranger replied. "You stay and have your coffee. Enjoy."

"I'm just going to be left here with the dog?"

"Oh. they forgot to tell you that, too, didn't they?" The woman stooped and patted the dog again. "He comes with me. That's what I came after you for." She gently eased the leash out of Serena's hand.

Serena couldn't help looking at her doppelganger in outright confusion. Nothing was making sense now.

The other woman shrugged. "You see, once we'd run the test with you, I then had my backup data hidden somewhere—or in something—where no one's likely to look for it. It's my key to immortality, so of course I need to be careful where I put it." She scratched behind the animal's ears, and for the first time Serena noticed a small incision in the dog's stomach where something had obviously been inserted. "Don't I, Data?"

She stood up and smiled at Serena, a sweet, understanding, yet sad grin.

"Enjoy your coffee. You've got about another five minutes before your system starts running down. You're only a short-term test run, after all."

The woman continued. "It was nice to meet you, if only for a while. You test models are so important. I won't forget you for a long time. And believe me, I have a very long time ahead of me." She smiled, then grimaced. "Although, even if I have all the time in the world to grow used to it, I don't think I'll ever love sugar in my coffee."

The woman whistled and called the animal over. "But, as you should know, I've always loved dogs."

Michael T. Schaper is an Australian writer who likes playing with words. A lot. He happily admits that speculative fiction is his guilty pleasure, even though he has also authored several non-fiction books and the odd textbook. This is all a refreshing break from a range of different professional roles, career-wise. These have included stints as a CEO, professor, business school dean, small business commissioner, regulator, company director, and even crayfish wrangling. No doubt some of this will make for fresh story fodder in due course.

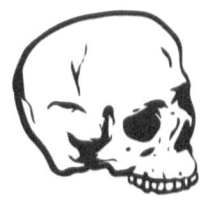

SOUL TRADERS

Darren Goossens

LIAM AND JODI liked InStream right away. They had *shopfronts* where customers could check out preproduction examples of the bodies they would inhabit when their flesh versions wore out and their memories were transferred. Jodi checked out Liam's body and vice versa. Liam liked what he saw, felt and smelled. He ran a hand over the Jodi-in-waiting; his fingers lingered on a hip.

"Better than the real thing?" said Jodi.

He raised his eyes. She looked content and satisfied—her version of glee.

"Not even close."

"Good answer." She kissed him.

Some things you can't get from virtuality, he thought.

InStream weren't the cheapest, but they had their own quarantined storage farms; Jodi had liked that and Liam had seen no reason to argue. The real-time experience data would be more secure and more stable, so that any consciousness reconstructed from the continuously synchronised data would be a truer copy of the original, ready for use and completely up to date. InStream also dropped their prices for customers who signed on for the long term. Jodi and Liam were in their late twenties, so that suited them perfectly, and they agreed to move their records over from their previous providers. They got their headsets fitted a few days later. Jodi did not like shaving her head, but within weeks the copper grids were invisible beneath her regrowing, equally coppery locks.

—

Did the knowledge that you were being synced make you more careless? Liam did not know, but soon after his thirty-second birthday, he did know that he should have paid more attention to the dark urine and pale stools. Prognosis followed diagnosis. Pancreatic cancer, stage four. The knowledge that he had another body to move into consoled Liam, and Jodi's pragmatism and support kept him from descending into fatalism, even as his visits to the oncologist came around ever more quickly.

Dr Wenger, a somewhat distant but essentially decent man, looked from his screen to Jodi and Liam, who sat side by side in stiff-backed steel chairs. Jodi, just arrived from court in her work suit and pumps, her satchel tucked under her knees, squeezed Liam's hand as if she could squeeze out the disease.

The doctor scratched his sparse grey hair and cleared his throat yet again. "We'll do everything we can." He coughed. "But I must suggest, and I know this may be a shock—please use this time to get your affairs in order."

Jodi's mouth dropped open; she then sat up straighter and nodded to herself. Liam knew that look; steel-plated determination.

Dr Wenger patted the air. "Yes, and you may want to look at freezing some sperm."

—

His treatment was by turns thorough, experimental, desperate and palliative—and always agonising, expensive and ineffective. Jodi sat beside him every moment until her annual leave and carer's leave ran out, which forced her back to work to pay for their mortgage and their plan with InStream. If the cancer had been vulnerable to force of will, Liam would have been out of the hospital weeks ago. Every night she slept in an armchair the nurses had moved into the space, delineated only by a ring of curtains, that was Liam's 'room'.

His cheeks sunken and yellowing, Liam lay on the bed. Jodi, in crumpled work clothes, sat by his pillow.

"You look tired," he said, then wished he had not.

She stared at him as if he had slapped her, then squelched that look.

He guessed at her thoughts. *Of course I'm tired. What am I supposed to do? Oh, he's sick, don't be angry at him.*

"Sorry. Please, Jode, go home. Get some real sleep. Sleep in your bed."

"Our bed."

"Yes, our bed."

"Not until you're there with me again."

Somewhere in the ward a steel bowl hit the floor. Somebody swore.

"Then sleep in the spare room." He smiled at his mild joke.

"It's terrible in that flat alone. Everything is *ours*." Her voice hardened. "It needs both of us. I can't be there now. I have to have you to come home to."

"I want to be there."

She leaned over and kissed him. Their tears ran together. Liam fought to wrap an arm around her. It would not respond how he wanted. The infuriating powerlessness brought reality crashing into the moment, killing it. Maybe he should just die and get the transfer out of the way. He hoped kissing her would be as intense when he was in his new body.

He heard the curtain draw back, then an understated cough.

The world swam back into focus. It centred on Dr Wenger, who stood at the foot of the bed.

"Jodi, Liam, it's time."

"Time?" said Jodi.

"I'm sorry. There's no way we can stop it now." He waited a moment. "I am sorry to have to be so practical at a time like this . . . are you okay to have this discussion? It doesn't have to be right now."

Liam looked at each other. "Go on," said Jodi, stiff like porcelain.

"We must begin formally coordinating with your provider. Have you spoken to them about this at all?"

"We contacted InStream a few months ago," Liam said. "They should be ready to start preparing my body and running all the checks."

"InStream?" said Dr Wenger.

"Yes? Why?"

"I'm so sorry."

—

29

InStream went broke a month later. That should have been fine—some big conglomerate would buy them up, maintain the service and make good on the policy. Then the stock market suffered one of its periodic moments of self-reflection. Investors went to ground.

Where are the tech billionaires when you actually want one? thought Liam while another needle went in.

The synced profiles of Liam, Jodi and about ten thousand other people became mere assets. What better to train an AI on than the entire life experience of a real human being, recorded in infinite detail on the assumption it would be programmed into a new body?

Eventually a buyer was found. A buyer, but not a service provider.

Transnational Training Data Services had other plans. InStream had promised not to share or on-sell the data, but when InStream ceased to exist but the assets remained, and were sold to TTDS, what then? TTDS had never promised InStream's clients anything, and decided to reuse the data without releasing it. Exclusivity only made the data more valuable. Regulation could not help—as usual, the legislators were decades behind, and preoccupied—so a desperate group of InStream clients began a class action. Jodi joined, but between watching her husband die and paying the bills, even she could not find the time or energy to watch the case slog its way across the legal landscape, an obstacle course she knew too well. The court of public opinion said InStream's customers got what they deserved—they were exclusive elites using a small, boutique supplier rather than going with BodyBuilders or International Transmigration Services. What did they expect?

TTDS might release the data next week, next year, next decade, if that became more profitable than keeping it—but would the bodies still be waiting? Would the data be pristine? Nobody could say.

TTDS did provide one service. They continued to sync Jodi and Liam to what had been InStream's system.

—

"Don't give up." Liam's voice was the strongest part of him, yet Jodi had to lean in to hear it. He did not have long. He lay, barely compressing the mattress, inert but for his lips and his eyes.

Jodi's hair was pulled back but the rest of her slumped. She was . . . simplified—utilitarian clothes, convenient flat shoes, a general-purpose expression of concern. Her hands rested on his arm.

"They've offered a deal," she said, her words as quiet as Liam's; they nearly disappeared among the squeaking wheels, clopping feet and indistinct, calm-yet-hurried voices of the hospital.

"A deal? So, the cost of doing the wrong thing has become slightly greater than the cost of doing a slightly less-wrong thing. Ha."

He tried for a cynical laugh but only a choking sound emerged; Jodi gasped and clutched his arm—hard—then drew back, appalled. Liam, embalmed in a chemical fog, hardly noticed.

"A deal," he repeated.

"Data and a body, each, the ones we contracted for from InStream."

"But?"

"They already own us. They want all future data as well."

"Do we get any say over what they do with us?"

She shook her head. "And—"

"Worse?" It was nothing but a breathy whisper.

"It's a lease."

"We have to *rent* our lives back from them?" He would have laughed.

"Something about 'cognition simulation technology that will benefit everybody'."

Everybody, Liam thought. *Every body. What does that even mean?*

"No," he said. "I've been expecting to die, really die, and I'm ready to."

"Don't say that. You're all dosed up. You don't mean it."

"But—"

"You might think you're ready, Li," she whispered, the words coming quickly now, "but I'm not. You won't be left behind. I will." She turned away and sobbed.

Was he being selfish? Was she?

The conversation ended. Thirty-seven minutes later, Liam died. She held his hand to the end, she kissed him, she told him she loved him. He would have done all those things in return if he could have. Liam died. Jodi crumpled.

—

There's no tunnel of light, no choir, no angels. Not unless it happens after the sync flatlines.

—

Jodi signed the deal for both of them. Mutual power of attorney, Liam recalled later. He got a new body and TTDS got their data.

She explained: "I know what you said, but you didn't have time to think it over. You were full of drugs. How could I do what you said when you've been feeling so hopeless for so long? Did you really know what you wanted? I had to make a call." He had never seen her plead before.

They stood in front of a wall mirror in a large fitting room. He was in his immaculate new body, a bio-electro-composite construction modelled on the flesh Liam, but lacking his fallen arches and receding hairline.

"This conversation and our internal responses to it are being sent to TTDS," Liam said.

"That stuff used to go to InStream."

They faced each other.

"InStream weren't going to use our data, our lives, to refine computer code." Liam's voice (*Liam's* voice?) voice sounded strange in his (*his*?) ears. He wondered if, being a machine, he could simply turn himself off.

"InStream went broke. This is what we've got. I love you, Liam."

He held up a hand and they looked at it. It was perfect. Not just a perfect copy of Liam's hand; absolutely perfect.

"I don't want—" Liam said. Thoughts moved around in his brain. What did he not want? "TTDS can put my data into their system." He spoke slowly, sorting through the words one by one. "Was there anything about TTDS putting *their* data into *my*—" but the thought ended. He paused, blank.

He smiled. He reached out to her. They hugged, they kissed. Jodi sighed and sank into his new, strong arms. She was so light. He calibrated his grip, slowed his breathing so it matched hers.

Of course, thought Liam. Transnational Training Data Services aim to benefit everybody. They will always have my best interests at heart.

Darren Goossens has published a handful of stories in a variety of magazines and anthologies. A former physicist, he is now a professional writer, editor and writing workshop facilitator.

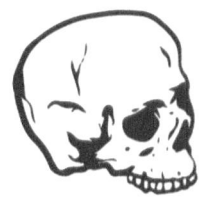

OF DEATH, CROWS AND
WITCHCRAFT

Fable Bea

CROWS ARE A moody bird. Those low, haunting cries replacing birdsong. To write a story about crows is to invoke a connection with death, the guts and the rot and the mood of it. Ravens have similar symbolic invocations, with the mood of death, but they carry an association with intellect, with the occult and witchery. There's a glint of intelligence in their eyes almost as bright as the snatched trinket in their claws.

But where something in ravens speaks of sophistication, trickery, dark omens, a sort of mastermind pulling unseen strings of fate to make a nest of ominous destiny, the crow seems scruffy and almost brutish by comparison. Their association is only with death, the dark and the gutsy messiness of it. A group of ravens form a conspiracy, but a group of crows becomes a murder.

So bring me a witch who chooses the crow over the raven. Bring me a witch whose magic stems from the rot and the guts and the bones. Bring me a witch crowned by a murder, who writes in blood and talon and finds power in the death of things. Bring me a witch who looks just as brutish and lost to the dark as crows might beside the ravens of their coven. Bring me a witch whose home is laced with picked-clean bones, whose familiars lurk in every tree and watch from every perch. Bring me a witch who sings to the low cries of the crows.

And who sounds just as haunting.

Fable Bea is the changeling child of an artist and a mad scientist. They enjoy bending the English language to their will, engaging their imagination in quiet moments, and telling stories of all kinds. They're fond of fantasy, tea, dragons, magic and worlds far beyond our own. This is their first officially published story.

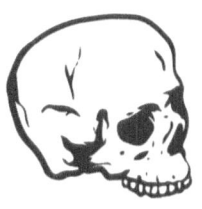

WRONG

Emma Gerts

THE AFTERNOON SUN poured through the open window, catching in sparkles on the dust motes that danced around burnished red-blonde hair like fireflies at dusk. Bird song drifted in on the breath of a breeze, spinning through the occasional counterpoint of a turning page. Her husband watched from behind the kitchen bench, pressing the tips of his fingers into the countertop until he could feel his delicate distal phalanges through the fragile flesh.

She *looked* normal. She *looked* like he remembered. The sunlight on the gentle curve of her cheek, shining through the delicate veins of her ear, a spiderweb tracery beneath skin and cartilage. Soft hair tumbling over a shoulder he had pressed his lips to a thousand times. Yet the hair down the back of his neck stood up in feral, hindbrain warning. His pulse pounded as his heart primed his muscles for flight.

She looked up, thumb resting on the page to keep her place. Her soft, familiar mouth curled into a smile. Small. A little unsure.

"Are you okay?" she asked in the voice he had heard every day for years. He made his face echo her smile, even though every muscle felt stiff with terror.

"Of course. Everything's fine."

—

The grief had been like a physical thing. Stones sitting amongst the cage of his rib bones. Taking up the space his heart had needed to beat. Crushing viscera to the sides. Leaving no space for breath. For eating. For living. The backs of his eyelids had become a movie screen for the imagination of her last moments. As if he had been there, his mind played the seconds like slides in a projector. Rain slick road. Delicate-boned fingers on the wheel. Headlights washing across cats' eyes like fallen stars on the asphalt. The moment the tyres lost their grip. The stomach dropping sensation of falling. Gravity shifting as up became down. The jarring suddenness of the tree.

He hadn't been with her. No one had been there as the steel and glass and plastic had torn and rent and ripped, and the oh-so-fragile flesh wrapping of a human being had been turned back into nothing more than meat. In the moments where the breath was being crushed from his lungs by the weight of her loss, he thought he knew how she had felt. Surviving felt like dying.

—

"I was thinking, maybe we should go to the farmers markets tomorrow?" she said. Her voice was raised a little, to be heard over the burble of the television reporting on the world's latest horrors, and the *splosh-slop* of the sponge as she washed a plate in the sink. His heart skittered in the way it did every time she spoke. She had barely finished her sentence before he was second-guessing the words. Were the farmers markets something she had liked before? Had they ever gone to the farmers markets before? *Before?* Was there some-thing off in the way she turned her head to look over her shoulder at him? Were her eyes just a little too flat, as if there was nothing behind them?

"Are you sure that's a good idea? What if someone we know . . . knew is there?" he said, and she turned towards him, drying her hands on a tea towel. Those hands, the interior structures of which he had memorised. The way the tendons connected to the bird-like bones. The way the light caught on the tiny hairs. The freckle on the knuckle of her third finger.

"We're a thousand miles from anyone who knew us, darling. Are you going to keep me locked in the house for the rest of my life?" she asked, the second half of the sentence dipping under the weight of the words. A genuine question hidden under the flippancy. A small line appeared between her brows. How many thousands of times had he kissed away that crease? Did she frown like that because she always had? Or because whatever was inside her was echoing the shape of her?

"No, of course not. We just need to be careful," he said, looking into her eyes and wondering what was looking back.

—

There hadn't been a single moment he'd been able to pinpoint as the one where the idea had come to him. It had been a slow coming to terms. The realisation that he simply couldn't continue. The breathless. Crushing. World ending. Pain. It was consuming him. Changing him. Her absence was a black hole, drawing the substance of him into it. Sucking his soul, his vital animation, into some unknowable void. It gnawed on his insides like rats in a cage. He knew he had to do something.

The choices had started to seem simple. He could join her. Or she could come back to him. The first option was a risk. He was a man of science. He wasn't sure if he believed, entirely, that there was somewhere beyond the bounds of life. If there wasn't, and he submitted to the darkness, there was no coming back. No second chance.

So it had to be option two.

—

It was a warm afternoon and the sun was like honey through the bright green of the oaks lining the park. He stood at a small distance as she inspected jars of jam arranged like ranks of soldiers on the white tablecloth. Her laughter rang like bells at something the red-cheeked woman at the stall said, gesturing with her graceful hands as she returned a comment. Laughed like she always had. The golden brown of her hair caught sparks from the sunlight and it was impossible not to remember gently washing it clean. Feeling the gritty dirt beneath his fingers. It was hard to open a grave without both of them becoming covered in earth.

She turned back towards him, tucking the newly purchased jar of preserve into the canvas bag over her shoulder. Her smile seemed so real, as if it were genuine.

But, every day that passed, the creeping sense of wrongness grew deeper.

The certainty that whatever had come back from behind the darkness was not what he had summoned.

"What a lovely woman. She makes all her jam by hand, you know? It looks delicious," she said, as she linked her arm through his, and he fought back the urge to flinch. Her skin was soft and warm, the underside of her wrist as satiny as he remembered it. Or was it a little too cool?

"Oh? Sounds time consuming," he said, searching for banality to cover his uneasiness. She shrugged her fragile shoulders, narrow beneath the light knit she wore. Had she been so slim before?

"I have plenty of time, now. Maybe I'll start making jam," she said, leading him off towards a stall selling soaps that smelt like flowers. His skin crawled as if it were full of spiders.

"Sounds great, darling."

—

It had been one part science. One part magic. One part faith. Desperation. Sheer force of will.

Before.

The Necromancer hadn't been a necromancer before the wet road and the sliding car and the stationary tree. He had been a man of science. A surgeon. Preoccupied with the mechanics of humanity. The tendons. The bones. The nerves and veins and skin and muscle that made a person.

After.

A person was more than the sum of their parts. Whether it was a soul or electrical impulses or something else. He could put a body back together but without that nebulous, intangible something, it would not be his wife. It would just be flesh.

The science took care of the physical. Months of careful work. Like a puzzle. Putting the pieces back together. Finding the broken connections. Repairing torn skin. Mending shattered bones. Painstaking. Time consuming. Fired from his job. Abandoned by his friends. Consumed by an obsession that had become his only lifeline. His only reason to exist. Forced by necessity to put his understanding of the intricate fabric of a person into the craft. In some ways, it was easier on the dead. He could take his time. In others, excruciating. Endless labour stripping him from the living. He put her back together, rebuilding her.

But that was the easy part.

The other part was harder. The intangible. The unreal. The vital spark that brought not just life but consciousness. He had stitched back her skin's perfect softness. Rebuilt her familiar curves. Soft hair and dexterous hands. But that would not replace her laugh. Her smile. The way she looked when he kissed her cheek. It took months. Finding the books that spoke of forbidden spells. Impossible magics. The forces that held the world in check. The magics that broke the laws of the universe. But he found them. Chased them down like a hound on the scent. Ferreted them out of the deepest, darkest corners of the web, from the dustiest reaches of the most protected libraries. He found the secrets to draw a soul back from the dead.

On a clear, cool night in June, the Necromancer brought his wife back to life.

—

He couldn't take it anymore. The days had become weeks, and weeks, months. The haunting had continued. He couldn't breathe when she was in the room. There was something different about her. Could not have told you what it was, if you had thought to ask, but he knew. When she spoke, her words were not her own. When she laughed, it rang false. The television shows she watched were unfamiliar. The meals she cooked, different. It wasn't just one thing. It was everything. It was a feeling. A sense.

Before the accident they had been normal. He had worked long hours in the hospital, her at the university. They had been loving, even if they had only seen each other for an hour or two in the mornings and a couple more some nights. Perhaps they hadn't watched tv very often, or eaten meals together more than once or twice a week. But it had been good. She had been a puzzle piece in a world that felt right.

Not now. The edges of the puzzle were jagged as broken glass. Grating against each other rather than slotting into place. They were together more than ever but he could no longer love her. Because she was not his wife. It was something else. Something that had come back from beyond. Something evil defiling his memory of her. He had broken the laws of living and death in his desperation and hubris and had created a hollow shell to invite in some evil. Hadn't he?

She was in the bath. She spent so much time in the bath now. Hiding from him? Avoiding him? Did she, did it, know he knew? Had he given her one too many lingering looks? Pulled back from her kisses one too many times? Had he given his doubts away?

He didn't knock on the bathroom door. Cold purpose filled him. The thing looked up as he opened the door, gave him a surprised, uncertain smile with his wife's face.

"Honey? What's wrong?" it said in her voice. The way the light glistened on the soft, smooth surface of her skin sickened him. You couldn't even see the cracks unless you knew they were there. He'd done a good job. Too good a job for it to be abused this way. He had made something perfect and it had become rotten.

"I'm sorry," he said as he came to the edge of the bath. The bubbles popped and crackled softly in the silence.

"Sorry for what?" it asked, and there was an edge of uncertainty in that familiar voice. He took a moment to admire the body he had pieced back together. It was so beautiful. But he had erred. He had made a mistake, thinking he could toy with the laws of the universe. This was his punishment.

"I'm so sorry," he said again. He wasn't talking to the thing in the bath, but to his wife, who he had failed. He put his hand on its chest, just below its collarbone, and pushed it beneath the water. Its eyes went wide in feigned shock. "I'm so sorry," he whispered, tears sliding down his cheeks. It thrashed, struggling, and he put his other hand on its head. Water sprayed across the room as its arms and legs grappled. Clawing at his arm. Heels squeaking against wet porcelain. "I'm sorry, my darling," he whispered as bubbles escaped in a rush from parted lips as it tried to scream. He had tried so hard. He'd wanted so badly to bring her back. To fix her. But he had to make this right, now. He had to send it back. Away. He held it down until the struggles spluttered, weakened. Became still. Until whatever had been inhabiting this perfect body was gone back to where it had crawled from.

The Necromancer had tried so hard to bring back his wife. But she had come back wrong.

He was sure of it.

Emma Gerts is a librarian, writer, and co-host of the writing and book related podcast What We Wrote. Emma started writing at 10 years old after reading *The Lord of the Rings* and becoming enraptured by the idea of creating such powerful stories. After meeting her bestie Esme 20 years ago at the age of 14, the pair started co-writing and have been doing so ever since. Since then, they have started their own podcast about their writing journey and will soon be publishing their debut novel, *Revelation*, under the pen name Alexis Roberts. Emma writes around her day job as an academic librarian, editing the podcast, riding and competing her horse, and spending time with her dog. This will be her first published story.

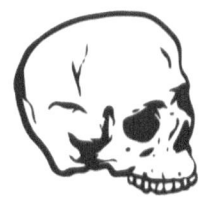

LET THE LAST I HEAR OF YOUR
VOICE BE MY NAME

Shana Cartwright

I DON'T WANT TO live again."

The declaration is met with silence. They sit alone in their bed-chamber, Adelina's razor-sharp amber eyes meeting Elian's baby blue. It is the longest night of winter, the height of Adelina's power, and once more they spend Elian's last night on the material plane to-gether. It is a night she cannot bear to spend with anyone else. Her palace is empty, but for them.

To answer such a declaration is to acknowledge some part of Elian, however small, wants to leave her. The thought is unbearable. She has never been alone. She does not even know how to imagine it. Her pulse thrums against her throat. She crosses her legs, brings her gaze to meet Elian's. She knows that look, and the knowledge pains her, for she knows he has decided.

"I just," Elian sits beside her, tucking her glossy black hair behind her pointed ear, "feel like I have lived all the life I was meant to live." His fingers linger at her neck with the delicate touch she had always loved.

"So you want to die?" she asks, sharply.

"No."

"Then?"

"I don't want to come back this time."

"You don't have a choice."

"There's always a choice." Elian has always known that. "Do you

45

remember what I told you about what I see before I come back?"

"I remember."

"Every time, I feel like I'm in a doorway. I can choose to go in, or come back to another life." He drops his hand from her neck to take hers. She doesn't resist, but her hand is limp in his.

"And you want to see what's behind the door? Without me?"

"You can come with me."

"I don't know if I can find you there."

"You've found me in every life I've lived, Adelina. Why not in death?"

"You can't know we even go to the same place."

"And yet, I do." She hates how decisive he sounds in this moment. He's always sounded like that—and usually she loves him for it. "How could it be any different?"

"I'm not ready."

"That's your choice."

"It's not a *choice* when you're forcing me to decide *now*," she snaps.

"Humans have never had the choice at all." He says it as if the fact that mortal life can be snapped away in an instant can balm the grief of her immortal soul. But, he knows the cruelty of that sudden loss: he fought in the war. He lost many without recourse or the opportunity to grieve. He knows the cruelty of only telling her when they have so little time left together. He knows, too, that otherwise she will be able to convince him to stay for another life. He could never deny her.

"We're not human—"

"I know—"

"But you're acting like you *want* to be one." Adelina's voice drips with resentment—not of him, for she could never do anything less than love him—but that he believes he must die. "Next you'll tell me life means nothing without its loss, that old piece of human propaganda. *We* were meant to be *more* than a meaningless ephemeral blip." That ephemerality—humans had always clung to it. Adelina resents it, especially now.

Elian is silent for a long time, stroking her knuckles with his thumb. "It wasn't meaningless to me." Elian says, slowly, softly. There's a hurt note in his voice. "Was it to you?"

"No." Adelina's eyes soften. "That's why I want another lifetime with you."

"I can't, Adelina."

"That's your choice." Her mirror of his words is corrosive.

It isn't lost on him that she doesn't ask *why*. She knows. She knows that each life has taken more and more from him. She knows that though he loves her, though she flourishes and blossoms with each of his passing lives, he has never found the cycle of death and life easy. She knows ever since they met in his first life—when he'd been drawn to the material plane to fight the war—that Elian has never *really* wanted to live. She knows that he is the only one of the two of them to ever face true death.

For Adelina, there has never been a door. She clings to life far too ferociously. Thus is the divergence of Fae and Spirit: that Fae shall always live and Spirit die again and again.

They both think the other is the stronger of them both.

"We can talk about it." Elian breaks the overlong silence.

"You've made up your mind," she says, weakly.

"Yes."

"And so, what's the point?"

"Because I care about you."

"Not now—"

"*Especially* now."

"No!" Adelina gets up, removing her hand from his. "You'd want to live for me—*with* me—if you did!" She yanks open her bedside drawer, pulls out a cold iron dagger. *True* death. That's what he wants, isn't it? She spins it in her hand, offers the hilt to him. "Well?"

He doesn't take it.

"I told you," Elian says, emphatically. "I don't *want* to die."

"You're choosing not to come back."

"It's not the same."

"It is!"

Gently, Elian takes her wrist, guiding her hand back down to the bed. "It's the Winter Solstice, Adelina. Let us have this last night."

Her eyes water, and she drops the knife. "I can't live without you."

"You've never needed me, Winter Queen."

"Don't call me that."

"I want to."

Tears still in her eyes, nervousness overtakes her cool demeanour. Though she fears she is wrong, she still believes he will come back. After all, he didn't take the knife. "If you truly will die tonight," Adelina forces out, "then let the last I hear of your voice be my name."

Elian closes his eyes, wrapping his arm around her, pulling her against his chest. He feels her pulse race under his arm. He feels the tug of his soul drawing away from this world. She feels it, too.

"I love you, Adelina."

"And so?" She whispers. For if he truly loves her, he must come back. He must *always* come back.

Every hundred years at midnight on the Winter Solstice, he has left her. By the morning, his soul returns, and every time she finds him. For her endless life is meant to always be with him. *Every* iteration of him. Every one of his lives will be with her.

And so, she will look for him tomorrow, just as she has for every death. For she knows he loves her, and so, she knows he will always return.

He does not reply.

Shana Cartwright is a speculative fiction writer living on Ngunnawal country, who's been filling notebooks with stories since she learned to hold a pen. She writes stories about the implications of the impossible becoming possible, and what happens when unfathomable beings love each other.

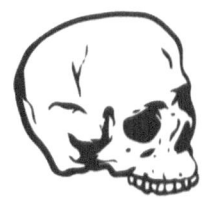

I SAW THE SAINT OF DEATH AT A ROCK SHOW

Elizabeth Pendragon

THE DINER DIDN'T have a name and wasn't really hers, but Jenny always thought of it as 'Jenny's Diner.' It was just easier that way.

It was a pocket of light and linoleum just off the highway. Nothing special, but plenty of people passed through on their way to somewhere better. Or somewhere worse, depending on the direction they went.

This evening, three teenagers came in; kids from the only town that could loosely be considered nearby. They set the bell chiming as they walked in without sparing Jenny a glance, heading for a booth in the back corner. Animated chatter floated back to her as they passed. The Ascension of a new Saint always made for a bountiful topic of discussion.

Jenny did a quick visual scan; the kids were the only customers. She felt some tension fall from her shoulders at that realisation.

She checked the coffee was hot enough before picking up the pot, tucked a cloth into her apron pocket, and made her way over to the booth where the three sat, bantering.

"Evening, kids," she said as she came to the table. "Who's for coffee?"

Only one, an acne-scarred young man, declined, so she filled the mugs of the other two and gave the table a quick wipe down before taking out her notepad.

"What can I get y'all?"

"Bacon and egg roll, thanks," said the one with shaggy hair and a septum piercing.

"Hash browns, please," said the girl in the denim jacket.

"Double hash browns," corrected the young man. "And a vanilla milkshake. Uh, please."

She rattled their order back to them, then headed back to the kitchen, humming along to the jukebox as she went.

—

"She new?" asked Rip, pushing aside their fringe to watch the waitress go.

"I guess," said Avaric. He picked absently at a pimple. "I haven't seen her here before."

"Maybe she doesn't usually work Thursdays?" offered Petunia. "It *is* very empty. Maybe there's something on in town and she's covering for the usual lady?"

Avaric just shrugged. Rip decided it wasn't worth pursuing.

"Whatever. I've got more important news anyhow."

They took a swig from their mug, giving the other two time to exchange a knowing glance.

"I went to a gig on Tuesday, and you'll never guess who I saw there."

Avaric groaned. "Not Marcie!"

"What? No!" Rip lowered their voice. "*Her!* The new Saint!"

Petunia and Avaric had been friends long enough that they made a habit of mimicking each other's expressions; they did so now, both of them adopting a wide-eyed look with one eyebrow wrinkled for a perfect surprise/scepticism ratio.

Rip basked in this for a few seconds before Petunia asked, "Are you sure?"

"Course I'm sure! Why wouldn't I be sure?"

"It's just . . ." Avaric hesitated, so Petunia ploughed forward.

"You've told some mighty tall tales, Rip," she said, bluntly, but in a way that said she quite liked those tales, really. "And this one sounds pretty lofty to me."

"Yeah," Avaric chimed in, relieved Petunia had more guts than he did. "I mean, why would the Saint of Death be at a metal gig?"

"It was prog rock, not metal!" Rip corrected, with offence. "And look, I know how it sounds. I know I exaggerate sometimes, yeah? But not this."

They put a hand into their shirt and pulled out their necklace, a plain silver chain and pendant. Avaric and Petunia knew it well; Rip never went anywhere without it. They gripped the fox-and-raven pendant in their fist and held it up.

"May The Mourner stop my heart if I lie. *I saw her.*"

Their friends exchanged looks. Rip could exaggerate, but they were serious about their faith. Anything they swore by the Goddess of Death was an oath they'd . . . well, die for.

"All right then," Avaric said, abandoning scepticism and leaning forward, elbows on the table. The light of sunset played red and orange across his face. "Tell us."

—

"It was Tuesday night," Rip began. "I was with the usual gang—and I swear, one day, I will get you two to join us. I swear it—but anyway, we met up, took Lee's pickup out to the spot. It was super low-key, right? Word of mouth only. So we drove a few miles and then turned sharp, just roared off the road into the desert and the dark.

"We found it, awesome little setup in the middle of nowhere. Some lights, big block stage, amps, generators, the works. Honestly, I don't remember who was playing, but I remember the music. It was so dark I could hardly see, but every dial was turned to max; I could feel the music in my bones, and it was like . . . the most real thing I've ever felt. Everyone was just dancing hard, partying, a few people were passing drinks around. I took a bottle from someone and had a swig, passed it on. And that's when I saw her."

"What did she look like?" Petunia asked, at the same time Avaric asked "What was she doing?"

Rip grinned. "What do you think, man? She was dancing!"

"The Saint of Death wouldn't dance!"

"I don't know what to tell you, dude! There was this epic bell solo happening and I looked over and she was dancing, just like everybody else."

"What did she *look like?!*" Petunia begged.

Rip paused to consult their memory (a rare occurrence).

"I mean . . . she just looked like a person, I guess."

Avaric looked disappointed. "What, not rotting or ghostly or anything? I thought she was cursed to 'carry death' or whatever. That's what I heard."

Rip waved the idea away.

"No, man! At least, I don't think so. She looked fine, just like . . . pale and gothy. Black hair, kinda short. Black clothes, but just jeans and a jacket, nothing crazy. I think she had some piercings, and a necklace but I couldn't see what it was. And she had some kind of tail clipped to her belt; fox, I think."

Petunia looked a little wary. "That's it? No, I don't know . . . halo, or anything?"

Rip shook their head.

"There was this moment, though, when everyone was dancing. It was so dark, right, but I could see her so clearly. I wasn't staring, okay? But when I looked at her next she was doing like, a spin, and she opened her eyes and . . . and she looked at me."

They rubbed the back of their neck.

"And then what?" Petunia urged.

"And then nothing. She looked me dead in the eye and sort of . . . smiled, I guess. Sadly. And then she went back to dancing."

Avaric gaped at them.

"Uh, that sounds *bad*, dude!"

"Hey, I'm here aren't I? Everything was fine."

Rip was done with answering questions, and to their good fortune this coincided with the arrival of their food. The group chorused awkward but polite thank-yous, and were left alone again.

Rip picked up their roll and took a bite. When they'd chewed enough to fit words in alongside the grease, they pointed a finger at Petunia.

"All right, Petal, your turn to talk. I know you've been sitting on something this whole time, I can see you fidgeting."

Petunia was looking sheepish, but in a confused, cranky sort of way. As though she were embarrassed but angry about it. Goatish, perhaps.

"Okay, look," she started. "I'm not saying you're lying, but I was going to tell you both that *I* saw her and—"

Avaric threw up his hands.

"Are you serious?!"

The other two stared at him.

"*I saw her!*" he said, jabbing himself in the chest. "I was willing to accept Rip's story—they were probably crossfaded as hell—but I didn't think you'd have one too, Petal!"

"But—" Petunia started.

"You think *I'm* lying?!" Rip cut in.

"Look—"

"Refill, anybody?"

The three of them cut off their argument and turned to look at the waitress. She seemed unaware she'd interrupted something.

"Um . . ." Avaric looked at the others, who shook their heads. "No, thank you."

"All right, give me a shout if you need anything."

And she left.

The three friends each waited for the others to talk, but nobody did. Eventually, Avaric took a sip of his milkshake and said, "Want to go first, Petal?"

She shook her head. "No. You go. I'm going to eat these while they're still warm."

"Cool," he said, then, "Thank you," after Rip gave him a pointed eyebrow-raise. Avaric took another sip of milkshake and cleared his throat.

"We open to a wide shot: the kitchen of NoodleFry, Tuesday evening."

Petunia and Rip shared an affectionate eye-roll. Rip may tell the odd fib, but at least they weren't a Drama student.

"It's dinner rush," Avaric continued in his thespian tone. "I'm on delivery orders, so I'm flat out at the stovetop, four woks at once and no slowing down."

He flipped back his mop of ruddy hair, picturing himself mid-toss of somebody's stir-fry, the stark kitchen light gleaming off beads of sweat on his forehead and his shiny assistant-manager badge. His friends knew this was a fantasy; he had to wear a hairnet in the kitchen.

"I'm a blur," Avaric continued. "Zoom in on my hands: they flash across vegetables, noodles, bottles of sauce—all of it passes through my fingers and into the pans with a grace not seen since Old Bazza worked the woks."

"Last weekend," Rip coughed, and Petunia smothered a giggle. Avaric frowned, but continued, unwilling to let his flow be disturbed.

"So there I was, a vision of stir-fry perfection, jamming along to

Seven Foot Screws on the radio. But then—tragedy! An impact shakes the scene . . .! Allison bumped my elbow on her way to the counter," he explained, when Rip and Petunia looked lost.

"Anyway. Refocus: in my hands, the oil. I'm mid-pour over a wok of Oodle-Noodle Special. The impact on my elbow shudders down my arm, and my rock-steady hands jerk. The oil flies. It flings itself over the wok, the stovetop . . . the open flames. And FWOOSH!"

He threw out his arms in a gesture which made both friends flinch, and rocked the milkshake glass dangerously close to tipping. Avaric righted it, then continued.

"Flames erupt in a wall of blazing heat. In them, my life flashes before my eyes: first words, first steps, first kiss, first—"

Rip cleared their throat. Avaric skipped ahead.

"I fall back and hit the floor. It's chaos all around me, but it's a blur, unreal. Eventually someone reaches through the flickering light and shadow of the flames to offer me a hand up. I don't recognise them, I assume they're a customer who came in to help. I go to thank them and . . . it's her."

Rip and Petunia leaned in.

"She was crazy pale, almost see-through, like a ghost. But her hand was solid. She told me I was okay. I . . . can't remember if I said anything. I just remember how warm her hand felt, and her eyes. They're different colours, like all the pictures. I think she was wearing pink eyeshadow." He shrugged. "And then I went home."

Rip and Petunia blinked at him for a while.

"My guy," Rip said. "You could've at least *texted!*"

"You almost died!"

Avaric shrugged. "I didn't want to worry you. Besides, I wanted to save the story for tonight."

He grinned, clearly pleased.

Petunia sighed. "You two, I swear."

"What did *I* do?" Rip demanded, incredulous.

"I wonder what she was doing there," Petunia continued, ignoring Rip. "I mean, does she even need to eat?"

"Do the other Saints eat?"

"No idea."

They all took a few minutes to finish food and wipe hands before Avaric prodded Petunia.

"Better give us your story now, Petal," he said. "Then we can all compare notes."

Petunia took a deep breath.

"Right. Well, um, you both know I've been dealing with some . . . health stuff, lately. It's getting better, but it's been tough."

She rubbed at her collarbones self-consciously.

"Anyway. I saw my doctor earlier in the week. The waiting room was really busy, which I thought was weird; don't people work on Tuesdays? Anyway. There were some crying babies and rowdy kids and cranky old people, and that terrible fake jazz they play on the radio. I was stuck waiting for a while, and I guess I ended up falling asleep, because my head went fuzzy and next thing I knew a huge sound jerked me awake. It gave me such a fright, I had a heart attack!"

She laughed; she was the only one.

"It was just my bag falling on the floor because I'd slumped over. Everyone looked so shocked, I felt really bad about it. I was looking around at all the surprised faces and I was blushing so hard, and then I saw one that was . . . smiling."

Petunia backpedalled.

"I mean, it was kind of a smile. But, a sad smile, kind of like you saw, Rip. It looked sympathetic, like she was trying to say 'Don't worry we've all been there!'"

"And it was her?"

Petunia shrugged.

"I think so. I mean, I'm pretty sure. She looked the same as you both described her, and how the pictures look on the pamphlets and stuff. One blue eye, one brown. Black hair. Pale. I can't remember what she was wearing, it might have been a dress. And some sort of necklace, and . . ."

Petunia looked suddenly very goatish again.

"Spit it out, Petal," Rip urged.

"She had a halo." Petunia huffed. "Or, a tiara, maybe? It wasn't float-ing so, I guess it was a tiara."

Avaric and Rip burst out laughing.

"A tiara?" Avaric scoffed. "I think you were dreaming, Petal!"

Petunia flushed a very dark pink.

"I was not!"

"Oh sure!" Rip hooted.

"She wasn't."

All three of them jumped and whipped around. The waitress was standing there, managing to look impassive but not entirely unthreatening.

Rip was still choking back their laughter as they asked, "Oh yeah? The Saint of Death wears a tiara, does she? And how would you know?"

The gaze the waitress fixed on them was sad and sharp, and sobered them up with jarring abruptness.

"For a bunch of kids who have seen a Saint first-hand, you don't seem to know much about her," she said.

The trio exchanged a round of glances, then looked back at her. Avaric said, "What do you know, then?"

She put the coffee pot down on the table.

"Her name was Alexandra Canaan, but when she took the Mourner's hand, she became the Saint of Death: the guide of the untimely dead to their hereafters. And yes, she wears a crown of thorns. One of the Mourner's gifts, along with her bells to toll the dead, and her flame to light the dark—but you knew about those already, don't you?"

There was a long quiet. Nobody answered her. The jukebox warbled its tinny tunes. Darkness had fallen, and there were no cars passing on the highway outside. There was only the diner, holding its occupants in its little bubble of light.

Petunia was the first to find her voice.

"How do you know all of that?"

The waitress shrugged. With that motion, the heavy atmosphere sloughed away, and the booth was bright and cheery again and the air smelled like bacon and eggs and coffee.

She picked up the coffee pot, and poured them all a fresh cup.

"For the road," she said simply, and made her way back to the counter.

—

The bell over the door jingled, the sound echoing sevenfold in the linoleum-lined space. It was a sound the Saint had gotten used to these past few weeks. Jenny, however, had not; Alex watched the waitress tense at the sound, going rigid for a few moments before turning to face her.

Jenny was nice. She was older, almost fifty. It was a common misconception—that you had to be young to have died "before your time."

Jenny had been kind enough to take up this post though, instead of passing on, and Alex was grateful. It made her job a little easier.

"What can I get you?" Jenny asked, wearing a tense half-smile.

"My usual please, Jenny," said Alex.

Jenny, anticipating this, punched the keys on the till.

"Hot chocolate with extra marshmallows, coming up."

The Saint put her hands in her jacket pockets, and glanced over to the booth where the three friends sat.

"Rough week," Jenny murmured, following her gaze.

Alex looked at her, offering a sad smile.

"Aren't they all." She sighed. "At least they have each other."

Jenny gave another of her half-smiles, and turned away.

The Saint of Death adjusted her thorns and turned towards the booth, where the boy was trying to throw a chip into his friend's mouth, and the girl was laughing at them both.

She did her best to walk slowly.

Elizabeth Pendragon is a lover of all things fantastical, gothic, and draconic, and enjoys exploring these themes through her writing. A storyteller of multiple means, she works in prose, poetry, and tabletop tale-telling to create and share her magical worlds. When she's not scrawling down ideas, you can usually find her trying out a new hobby or cuddling her cat/familiar, Salem.

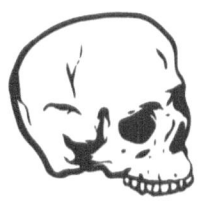

THE BONE TRADER

Lee Cope

THE REEKING SLIME that was once flesh has been safely buried. The woven mats are laid out neat and careful. Your gloves are heavy, your apron thick, and your own breath mingles with the near half-dozen essential oils soaked into your mask. You gently pass river water mixed with strong liquor over your grandmother's bones to slough off the last of her flesh, and gather your family to scrub her clean.

A week after she has been dried and sorted, you stand before the woods. The box of your family's bones is heavy on your back, the straps digging even through your thick clothes. You know not to wish it was lighter. When that wish comes true, and it soon will, you know you will wish it hadn't.

Nana's sister avoids touching the box as she hugs you goodbye, and does not tell you to wait just a little longer. She does not say that she wishes her sister's bones weren't leaving without hers.

—

To enter the forest, you first must trade with the standing stone guarding the crossroads. It says nothing to you, but its companions do: three tiny stones with arms like flint flakes roll and bounce towards you, chanting "Trade? Bargain?" in raspy unison. You place your box gently on the ground, ignoring the faint chill as the soft breeze hits the sweat on your back and the way three tiny stone noses are pressing insistently against your thigh.

You know the rules: the forest creatures will accept an offer too high but never too low. They never accept the fourth offer, nor any after. You also know what price others paid to pass these crossroads, much more detailed than any account of the creatures beyond. Nevertheless, your hands shake as you open a drawer.

"My mother's brother," you recite, lowering the snapped half of a curved bone to the height of your knee so the little stones can see it. "This rib snapped inside of him, and would have replaced his breath with blood, save for our farm dog running for his father, and his father running for the doctor."

Your uncle's rib is snatched from your hands so fast you feel only a breeze on your skin. The three pebbles tumble back towards the standing stone. And you lift the box back onto your shoulders, passing the crossroads into the forest.

—

The trees have grown close and tall around you, their bark pitted like rusting armour. The path twists between them, well worn, but there aren't enough feet in all the villages surrounding the woods to entirely keep the roots back. Ahead, you can hear running water, and you think of the near-empty bottle in your bag, nestling next to your food and the first aid box.

Something steps into the path in front of you, and you stop sharp, your box pressing hard into your back. It moves like a grazing deer, despite its stiff bark-and-moss skin. If it stood straight, it would probably be half again your height, but its question-mark back brings your faces level. Its eyes are huge, flat, and its chin curves towards its chest so steeply that from here, you cannot see its mouth.

"I greet you, traveller." Its voice sounds like it learned your language listening to songs, not speech. "Walk where you will, but if you want water from the river, then I will have a toll."

Its eyes do not—perhaps cannot—move in its face as it watches for your reaction. You try not to give one, but you're certain it has seen your shoulders rise, your hand clench on one of the straps holding your box to your body.

This is not what you were taught. Your family said water is the only thing in the woods that cannot be owned. You do not answer the creature immediately, slowly kneeling and placing your box on the uneven road.

It watches, waits. Its bark body is stiff, and there is no way to read the set of its face or shoulders, or the expression of those unblinking eyes. You cannot argue; you cannot risk offending it if you're wrong. Nor can you risk waiting for the next river to refill your bottle.

Perhaps you can at least minimise the damage. If it must accept any bone above the value of what it offers, then it ought to accept a mere token for something it doesn't own in the first place.

Nobody has ever learned for certain whether the worth or the bone is in its size or its story. You try to select one that hasn't much of either. This one: a bone a bit longer than your longest finger, curved like a bike's handlebar. "My father's father's mother's uncle," you recite. "His collarbone. It was with him when he was born and with him when he died."

Just like the rib, it is gone from your palm without the creature ever touching your skin. It retreats wordlessly from the path.

At the stream, you fill both your canteen and your belly, and take a moment to clean your face and simply breathe.

—

The trees are now so tall that you have not known for many hours whether it is day or night. They have expanded in every dimension, their roots as tall as your knee in places, the grooves in their bark wide and deep enough that you could lose your whole arm in one. The twilight turns them into jagged, shadowy pits. You keep to the centre of the path, both to avoid the roots, and because you suddenly cannot stand the thought of your hand near that bark.

You have spent many bones on tolls, some for guidance, one to buy your safety. As you push the thought of the gradually lightening load from your mind for what seems the thousandth time, you hear footsteps that aren't your own. They cannot be an echo: the gait is different to yours.

In the permanent twilight between those huge trees, it feels like you wait near half an hour before you loosen your jaw enough to call out.

"I don't mean to trespass," you say.

"I claim no toll from travellers. Walk where you please." The inside of a winter cellar, cold and full of foods suspended in their own juices somewhere between freshness and careful rot, would sound like that, if it had a voice.

You have nothing to say. One tree trunk passes, then another. The footsteps do not alter their gait.

The voice speaks again. "I have information. You could buy it, if you chose."

"I don't need it. But thank you for the offer." The first half is less true than the second, but something in you insists that you shouldn't trust this creature, even if a trade binds it to honesty.

"Then, a diversion?" There's an edge to the voice now. A hunger.

"Thank you, but I'd prefer to just go on my way," you say as politely as possible. "Since this part of the road isn't owned."

This time, when you stop speaking, it is not only the voice by the side of the road that falls silent, but everything. The so-distant birdsong, the low creak of huge tree trunks, all have disappeared. There is only the near-deafening rush of your own blood through ears desperately seeking sound.

An invisible foot hits the ground by yours. The voice, so close that you are genuinely surprised not to feel breath on your cheek, says, "I never said this road was not mine."

Your neck *hurts* as you tense, your body pulling sideways. The weight of your bone box makes you tilt, stagger, and as you put your hand out to catch yourself, nothing meets it. Your knees hit a tree root hard enough that your stomach clenches as the sharp ridges hit tendon, but you dare not stay kneeling to check them over.

Standing is near impossible. Though you can see the path clearly, you find yourself weaving erratically from side to side, catching your feet on roots that you thought you stepped over. Even on the flat ground, the path twists under you and sends you stumbling.

And then the voice, still right by your ear although you never heard it move: "A diversion?"

You have no choice. You nod, because your throat is stuck to itself and your breath is coming too hard for you to speak.

The footsteps resume, once again somewhere in the trees by the side of the path, and the voice continues, "The rules, then."

"The rules," you choke out, feeling you must say *something*.

"One," it says, in its cellar-shelf voice, "Keep walking. You may choose your pace but not change it. You may not run. Two, you must answer my questions. Three, for every incorrect answer, and for every answer you fail to give, I claim a token from that box. Do you understand?"

Not agree. Understand. You do. You nod.

You pick your foot up and put it down cautiously. The roots stay in their places now, and the path no longer seems to twist ahead of you. You take another step, and then another: a quick pace, but a steady one.

The footsteps remain slow and deliberate, keeping pace with you. You picture this creature in human skin. It would be striding, its hands clasped loosely behind its back. You can imagine those hands in vivid detail—veined but not wrinkled, nails meticulously scraped clean—but hard as you try, no face will resolve into the space above its iron-crisp collar.

"First question. What do you travel towards?"

"I am forging a path through the woods so that my family, and other families like ours, may travel it in the future." The answer you were taught comes out of your mouth before you can think.

The box on your back rattles in a way your steps cannot possibly have caused. You jerk to the side, but there is nothing to jerk away from. By the time you react, it is already over. You didn't feel the weight of the box change, but the knowledge is in your blood, sinking into every chamber of your heart. Something has been taken.

"Wait," you say. "What I *mean* is that the destination isn't important. What matters is that after I have done it, it will be possible for others. That goal, not a place, is what I travel towards."

"Semantics."

"You can't blame me for misunderstanding." Neither the reediness in your voice nor the way your teeth are stripping flakes from your lower lip give your words the force you wish they had.

A second. Two.

Something in you threatens to rise into your mouth when the voice says, "Very well. I shall ask another. Answer it, and I'll return this bone to you, and shall be more considerate with my questions."

You only nod.

"Next question: thinking back to every bone taken out of your box. Did you pay a fair price for all the things they bought?"

Your liver presses down against your intestines, your lungs and heart lifting into your throat, all to get away from the clawing hole that exists where your stomach used to be. You try, nevertheless, to say anything but the words you know to be true. "I do not regret any of the bones I spent."

"That does not answer my question," the voice says. "And this time I do not believe you misunderstood."

Silence drags. You place one foot in front of the other, measuring your pace. Finally, the words leave you. "I cannot—I don't know."

You don't know whether it is better or worse that the voice does not laugh at you. "Tell me of this thing I have taken from you," it says.

You're about to protest that you don't know which bone it has, but before you can, the image of it appears in your head and you find the recital drawn from your throat. "My mother's father's sister," you say. "A bone from her spine. She was born with it sitting out of place, and so she wore stays all her life. They made her sit like a queen. Mother remembers that some days, she preferred to walk than sit, so she used to crochet while slowly pacing in front of the fire. Mother still owns a hat she made that way, and uses it on cold mornings."

A pause. "Very well," the voice says. "Next question."

You remember suddenly that you agreed not to run.

—

You have now been walking alone for some time. The trees are so big that each one seems like a wall. You have not seen natural light for days, you are sure of it, and yet the path is well-lit compared to the twilight where you found the bodiless voice.

Your legs are shaking. Your lip is scraped raw. Every time you move, the bone box rattles emptily and you try not to calculate how many generations it will take to replace what you have lost.

As you look up and see another standing stone, a short wooden table before it, this one marked with a faintly carved face, you know with a sensation between resignation and nausea that you must prepare to lose another bone.

It tilts forward, inviting you closer. You kneel, gently place your box on the ground next to you, sit at the little table. For a moment, you lean on it, forehead pressed into the cool wood, eyes closed. Eventually, the stone interrupts.

"Do you wish to pass?" it asks.

Your chest hurts, and it is only after your teeth press into your lower lip that you remember it will hurt. You are too tired for niceties. "May I ask a question first?"

"Yes."

"How much of the path lies beyond this point?"

Another strange tilt. You wonder if it means to lower its head without a neck to bend. "I cannot say," it replies.

You nod. You never should have expected anything else, should you?

Fingers heavy, moving as if every joint is swollen, you search through your box, weighing up your remaining bones. The one you choose might be too much, but you cannot think any more. "Is this enough?" you ask, presenting a femur, pale and heavy in your hands. "It belonged to my father's mother's sibling's son. On it he walked, carried his own children, danced with his husband, and in the later years of his life, his cat sat on this bone of an evening while his children read to him."

You brace for the bone to be snatched, but nothing happens.

"This payment is not sufficient," the stone says.

Suddenly, you cannot breathe. Every place where your eyes touch their sockets is stinging. You try to ignore that, and the way your head has begun swimming, as you search for another bone. You pull out one that is round and familiar. You held it and washed it not so long ago.

"This is my Nana's skull," you croak. "She was a scholar. This skull held the knowledge she passed to my mother, to me, to her students. I rested my head against this skull as she traced words on the page for me to learn when I was small."

You wait. Brace.

But again, the stone says, "This payment is not sufficient."

The skull rattles as you fumble it back into the drawer. What else? You have only one more chance. What else do you have?

You stare at your hands for a long time.

Your feet have to carry you. But your hands . . . you can afford this, right?

Cooking knife, cloth, alcohol. You make sure the blade is clean and sharp, and the standing stone watches you do it. It watches you lay your left hand flat on its tiny table, and search with the heel of the blade for the notch in your knuckle that indicates the joint. Your stomach rises to your throat, but that's alright. There wasn't anything in it to lose anyway.

You rise to your knees as you lean on the knife, hoping more of your weight behind the cut will make it quicker. You pull your hand back fast, and the cloth soaks through almost as soon as you press it to the wound.

You slide the last two bones of your finger across the table.

"They're not cleaned," you say, in a voice that barely sounds like your own.

Instead of answering, the stone asks, "Why did you offer me this? What makes these bones more valuable than those that remain in your box?"

Keeping pressure on the wound is starting to make your stomach turn again. You can't think. But you only have one chance to answer this question.

So you recite, "My bone. The last finger on my left hand. It has never held a child of its own, nor has it taught a skill, or made any great sacrifice . . . until it was removed." You take a breath, which seems to stick on every fold inside your mouth and throat. "But if none of those things are valuable enough to pay for my passage, maybe this is." You tilt your head up and look directly into the stone's carved face. "It belongs to a body that has not yet ceased to live."

A moment, and then you must have blinked, or perhaps your mind wandered for a moment. The finger is gone. The carved face has turned, ever so slightly, toward the path into the trees. "You may pass."

Blood is dripping into your lap. Your head is already swimming, imagining the sting of your disinfectant, and the ache of wrapping it up. But you must. You must continue.

You already bought passage, after all.

Lee Cope is a writer, game designer, Purveyor of Fine Falsehoods, and one half of Whimsy and Metaphor Enterprises. It likes making beautiful things strange and uncomfortable, and uncomfortable things beautifully compelling. Once upon a time, it had a hope of leaving academia, but that opportunity has long since passed. So far, it has been nominated for two Aurealis Awards and one Otherwise Award. You can find its self-published fiction at whimsyandmetaphor.com, as well as links to its social media.

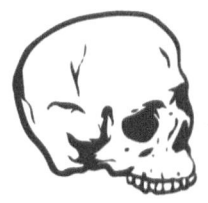

Applied Ethics for the Apprentice Necromancer

C.Z. Tacks

Y AN ISN'T LOOKING for mysteries. For once, he's not even looking for corpses. After six months of wearing his fingers to stubs making stone pins and glass needles and the other tools of the trade, Yan has at last been given leave to explore the underpalace. The layered maze of basements and dungeons and storerooms beneath the shining seat of royalty above, home to scavengers and servants and Yan, new-minted apprentice to the Master Necromancer and worst of both worlds.

Naturally, Yan finds a mysterious corpse.

In life it was a man about Yan's age. Even slack, the face is severe; stern brows, hooked nose. None of the sagging of the mouth or staring open eyes of the unembalmed dead, which unsettles Yan. The corpse is filthy—worse than Yan when his boss first scooped him up—but no visible wounds. Yan backtracks to the storeroom door and finds the remnants of a serious ward, eaten away by time and rodents. By the layers of dust covering the corpse, the wards, and the floor, no one has come back for it in a long time. The *real* mystery is why there's no accumulated years of death-stink for Yan to choke on.

Yan puts his hands on its neck and nose to feel for signs of life. He finds none.

Yan's boss loves a sneaky test as much as she loves funerals. It's how she chose Yan; left a pile of bodies in an alleyway and watched as the bone-grubbers crept out and picked them over. When Yan pulled the one comatose curse victim out from among the dead, the Master Necromancer promoted him from piteous urchin to official apprentice. It's too soon for another promotion, but Yan's boss might want to keep him on his toes. Or perhaps she's checking on his homework; this might be something Yan would understand if he'd spent less time exploring and more time reading the *Principia Ethica Necromantia*.

Yan hedges his bets and hauls the corpse back to his rooms.

All the apprentices get their own laboratories. Yan's has a big wooden table, pitted and scarred; a spindly three-legged stool; a sturdy washstand; a drain in the sloping floor; a shelf of books his boss wants him to read; a case of necromantic tools; and two bespelled lamps. When the Master Necromancer showed it to him, Yan thought it was her idea of a prank, even before he found out he had a whole second room with a bed and a wardrobe and a second washstand and a real silver mirror. When she told him about the clothing allowance, he swooned.

The corpse goes on the table. Yan puts his hands on his hips and stares at it, hoping for inspiration.

None comes.

Well, Yan's boss tells him he's an experiential learner. Yan takes his blurry memory and dangles it by the ankle until some useful experience falls out of its pockets.

Yan's first family, the dead one, had rules about proper treatment of corpses. Yan doesn't know most of them; it was one of many things that, in a show of staggeringly poor foresight, his family meant to teach him once he was grown. He remembers a shroud of undyed linen and smoke from tallow candles. He remembers his tiny child's hands offering up a dripping sponge; cold water running down his wrists and soaking his sleeves.

He's not sure if palace people have the same funeral customs. His boss took him to watch the cremation of the corpses from his entrance exam, but he has no idea what she did with them between the pile and the pyre.

The memory lingers.

Yan's washstand refills with clean water every day, and whenever he's low on lye soap or clean rags, more appear in their proper places. He can't sense a spell, but he's never caught a servant in the act either.

He wets a rag and rubs experimentally at the corpse's grimy hand.

The filth, he determines, is post-mortem: cobwebs, dust, the dark greasy schmutz that accumulates in the underpalace like worms in mud. Cheered, Yan sets the rag aside and starts undressing the corpse.

The clothes are finer than Yan had thought at first; the outermost layer is colourful brocade under the carpet of dust. He finds twin slices in the outer and inner robes, each edged with brownish bloodstains; the tapering suggests a stabbing. Yan sticks his fingers through and encounters only cold skin stretched over the swooping curves of the ribcage. When he peels them back, there's a thick white scar, too old to be the cause of death.

"I can understand keeping the cuts in the clothes," Yan tells the corpse as he strips off the rest of the clothes. "Morbid little memento. Whatever. But the blood? That's just gross."

Yan finds another bloodstain on the corpse's left hand, a faint crusting of brown at the tip of its first finger. He almost misses the culprit: a black glass needle jammed beneath the corpse's fingernail. Inserted antemortem, but only just; there's hardly any inflammation.

Yan uses a pair of tiny silver forceps to draw it out and sets it carefully in a dish for later examination. It shatters, of course. One of the fragments slices across Yan's knuckles. He drops the forceps and almost jams the wound into his mouth before he remembers it had recently been in a corpse and returns to the washstand for soap instead. He and the corpse could both use a scrubbing.

It's while he's sluicing the suds from his new roommate that Yan's brain catches up with his eyes.

The black glass needle is a spellcrafting tool of precisely the kind Yan has spent the first half-year of his apprenticeship turning out by the dozen. Only necromancers leave their tools inside the dead. It was inserted beneath the fingernail; not the most efficient point of entry, but somewhere only a necromancer would look unprompted. The grime told of months or years spent untouched, and the clothing told of a bloody wound, yet the flesh was unmarred by violence or decay. The corpse didn't even void its bowels, that final indignity which nothing prevents—save, perhaps, some serious magic.

Yan washes his hands again before he sits down and puts his head in them.

If he's read the signs aright, his mystery corpse was struck down by a necromancer of subtlety and strength. Given that Yan found it down in the dark where she keeps her apprentices, the likely culprit is the Master Necromancer. And Yan has brought the evidence of her crime home with him.

"At least you won't be lonely," he tells the corpse. "My boss is gonna kill me."

—

No one ever knocks on the Master Necromancer's door. Yan used to fret about someone barging in unannounced, but then he realised none would dare intrude upon his boss without an appointment. At least, not for anything less than the ocean opening and all the dead walking out.

At the appointed time, the pair of skeletal servitors on either side of the door stir, silk thread and jade pins taking the place of their long-lost ligaments and muscles. One opens the door just long enough for Yan to walk in.

The Master Necromancer looks up from the disassembled skeleton on her desk to study him. Yan studies her right back.

Yan's only ever seen the royal bastards' collective father on coins, but that's enough to know none of them take much after their mothers. They all have the same strong brows and beaky nose, though they wear them differently; some menacing, some melancholy. Yan's boss isn't that old—maybe mid-thirties—but the features make her look ancient and implacable. Even the gentle light from the big window in the western wall can't soften her.

Yan recalls those features very well; he saw them on his basement corpse just this morning.

Could it be the corpse is an unknown kingly by-blow? Or a known one, even; they do seem to drop like flies. Yan isn't sure if that makes his boss more or less likely as the murderer. She has some fondness for most of her surviving half-siblings.

Yan's boss gestures to a chair with an open hand.

Yan sits and asks, "Nonia, do palace people wash corpses?"

"You did not hear?" Yan's boss steeples her fingers beneath her chin. "I am Octavia now."

"Congratulations," Yan says. "Or condolences. How many siblings is that you've lost?"

"I have never lost a sibling," Master Necromancer Octavia says. "That would be careless. Half-siblings, though? This makes four."

She smiles.

Yan doesn't know what to do with his boss' smiles. It'd be one thing if they were the dead-eyed sharkish smiles the other palace-dwellers use, but Octavia's are warm, almost maternal, inviting him to share her joys and jests. They make Yan's guts churn.

"Master Healer Tertius must be pretty embarrassed right now," Yan says. "So many inexplicable illnesses in his family, and not a cure to be had."

"He is now Master Healer Secundus," Octavia says. "I imagine it consoles him."

Which probably means the Master Healer is dabbling in death curses. Yan isn't well-versed in the ways of the royal court, but even he can tell that's an outright insult to the Master Necromancer. He might have a better grasp on these things if someone would just explain it to him, but no one's willing to risk being overheard.

"You gonna do anything about that?"

"Yan," Octavia says patiently, "Secundus is my half-brother. A child of royal blood. Entrusted with the sacred duties of the Master Healer. And we cannot prove his involvement in the disappearance of Primus Maximus, or the illness of Secundia Major, or—"

That's not a no, but it also seems a dangerous line of thought to let the Master Necromancer pursue, so Yan proffers a distraction. "Wait, you didn't answer my question. Corpse-washing: yea or nay?"

"Not ritually," Octavia says, "but visible soiling would be removed before cremation. How do you find the *Ethica*?"

"It's fine," Yan lies.

Octavia pins him with a look as sharp as a black glass needle. "A test, then. Why are skeletal servitors preferred?"

"*Ethica* says you gotta."

The Master Necromancer arches a single eyebrow. The weight of the stare forces breath out of Yan's lungs. It implies he should do better, quickly.

Yan scratches the back of his neck. Experiential learning suggests an answer: "People get real mad if they recognise your puppets."

Octavia smiles again, which lifts the crushing weight from Yan's chest but also makes his skin crawl. "For your own sake, perhaps re-phrase that when you venture outside of the underpalace."

"Don't seem like it should matter," Yan grumbles. "The dead don't care."

"Our ethical standards rarely consider the needs of the dead," Octavia says. "After all, they have none. Our duty is to the living. We offer comfort and avoid undue distress, even when it may be inconvenient. When you read the *Ethica*—"

Yan winces.

"—you might observe that common thread." Octavia places a proprietary hand upon the skull on her desk. "A necromancer owes duties to their servitors akin to those the master of a house owes to their household."

"Household covers a lot of ground," Yan says dubiously. "Is servitors more like an apprentice or a spouse?"

"Depends on the servitor," Octavia says slyly.

Yan snorts out a laugh despite himself, then realises an opportunity to eke out an answer.

"Do people ever ask you for the other way? Stop their dead from getting gross?"

"Rarely," Octavia says. "Decay and death are natural allies. Assuming I am present at expiry and act at once, I might stop the rot for a week or two. In winter, I might do better, but covering the body in snow would be cheaper and more effective."

Yan allows himself tentative optimism that he hasn't incriminated his boss by finding her victim and is, as such, at no greater risk of being killed and made into a servitor than he was yesterday. Of course, that leaves the new problem of figuring out who he *has* incriminated.

"Hypothetically," he says, forming each word with slow caution, "could *anyone* do that? Make a body that never rots?"

"Oh, yes. Incorruptibility is quite achievable, if you follow one simple rule." This time, Octavia's smile does have a touch of the shark about it. "Don't start with a corpse. Decay is no ally to the living."

—

Yan leaves with instructions to take a copy of *Case Studies on the Applications of Incorruptibility and Related Workings* from the Master Healer's library, read it, and report back to his boss after supper. Yan skims the first few chapters. A curse-induced coma. A stasis spell to allow recovery from mortal wounds. A charm to slow the symptoms of consumption. That's more than enough for Yan to place Master Healer Secundus as his hypothetical corpse-maker, and homework abruptly strikes him as a dangerous occupation. He takes the book back down to his laboratory and dumps it on his table.

His unoccupied table.

Yan stares at the place where the corpse ought to be.

"Don't panic," he tells himself firmly. "Corpses don't walk off unless someone makes them."

Then he sprints out into the halls of the underpalace.

He darts back to the room where he found the corpse, even though corpses don't have memories or care about where they're interred. When that does not produce Yan's corpse, Yan bolts towards the lower levels and crashes into a young man who takes him by the shoulders and asks if he's all right. The man is a head shorter than Yan and wearing the robes of an apprentice necromancer, and the thought of Octavia finding out he lost a whole corpse lights whole new fires of panic beneath Yan's feet, so he just shoves out of the man's grip and keeps running.

Then he realises the only thing worse than Octavia finding out he lost a corpse is Octavia finding out he lost a corpse and *didn't tell her immediately*.

Yan skids to a stop with heaving chest and trembling limbs. Then he turns around and races towards his boss' study.

He's sweating and gasping by the time he arrives. The servitors on Octavia's door have multiplied from two to six. The new ones have thin steel chains in place of silk thread and iron nails in place of jade pins. Not genteel palace servants: these are built tough, the kind of servitor that can attack or defend. Yan stumbles and stops on the threshold, eyes darting from grinning skull to grinning skull.

If he's being honest, he wouldn't have been game to knock even without the new servitors, but the bony bruisers don't help.

One of the silk-and-jade skeletons opens the door.

Yan freezes.

The desk and half-finished skeleton remain. He can't see Octavia, but the shadows in the room suggest she's standing by the window, just out of view from the door.

"Yan," the Master Necromancer says. She sounds exasperated, as if Yan was hesitating over unfinished homework and not losing an entire corpse. "Don't hover like some gawking peasant."

Yan steels himself. She can't do worse than kill him, after all.

"You knew I was a gawking peasant when you picked me up," he says, and slinks inside. Octavia is indeed standing by her window. It's later than Yan had realised; the setting sun makes the Master Necromancer into a robed silhouette.

"That's the one," another voice says.

Yan spins around so fast he trips on his own robes and cracks his hip painfully on Octavia's desk. The loose bones rattle and jump at the impact, clicking against jade pins shaped by Yan's own hands.

The other person in the room is positioned so that, should the door open, he'd be hidden behind it. Yan takes in the clothes and the height and realises that this is the other apprentice Yan collided with in his frantic dash through the underpalace. The robes don't fit him; tight in the shoulders, and longer than they ought to be.

Octavia steps away from the window. The man blinks as the light of sunset falls across his face, and Yan recognises him all over again.

The basement corpse rubs the back of his neck and offers a sheepish smile. "I borrowed some clothes. I hope you don't mind."

Yan has to bite down on two of his knuckles to keep from swearing or shrieking or both.

"Yan," Octavia says, taking her place on the other side of her desk. "This is my elder half-brother, Primus Maximus. Primax, this is my apprentice, Yan."

Yan removes his knuckles from his mouth and cautiously eases into his usual seat. "Not to tell you your business, boss, but that man ain't more than twenty."

Octavia steeples her fingers. "I take it," Octavia says, "that you have not had time to read those case studies."

Yan hunches his shoulders. It's only been a few hours; what did she expect? "I skimmed them."

Octavia sighs. "If the current Master Healer Secundus had, in his youth, assaulted Primax—"

"He stabbed me!" Primax pats his side, where the robes hide his scar. "His aim was true, though he failed to reach anything important. Poor form undermined him; if he had kept his wrist straight, he could have done it. One ought not set a healer at the tasks of an armsman."

Yan recalls that he stripped Primax naked and bathed him, running his grubby peasant hands all over that royal skin. He wheezes like his own lung has been punctured and put his head between his knees. Octavia may not kill him, but the cringing humiliation might. Maybe that's why the fancy folk call it mortification.

"And if, in theory, I had found Primax as he was bleeding out," Octavia continues doggedly, "I might have used a necromantic needle to improvise a spell of incorruptibility. Such a working would allow Primax to heal from his wounds, though it would be slow; nigh on ten years." She abandons the hypothetical with an exasperated huff and adds, "It would have been less time if he had been seen to by a chirurgeon or a healer, but under the circumstances, I imagine you might understand my reluctance."

"What was the plan?" Primax demands, so boldly that Yan flinches on his behalf. "Leave me there until the rest of the family was senescent?"

"I had meant to smuggle him out when Secundus next left the palace," Octavia says, without so much as an eyelash twitching towards her brother. "But you, my dear apprentice, removed the needle that kept him from *interfering*."

Yan uncurls just in time to see Octavia give Primax a look that might slice a lesser man open. They really are siblings.

"How're you blaming me?" Yan asks, half-hysterical. "If you'd warned me not to interfere with the basement corpse—" He cuts himself off, then swings his head around to glower at Primax. Of the two, he is by far the safer target for Yan's wrath. "And you look fairly glum for a guy I raised from the dead this morning!"

"I hope I don't seem ungrateful," Primax says. "It's only that—he's Secundus now, is he?—Secundus has had a decade to really refine the art of murder. Sadly, I lack comparable experience in keeping myself alive. It might be best if I stay dead."

"Why, Primax, I believe you have struck upon a solution," Octavia says. "Congratulations, Yan. You have your first servitor."

Primax gives Yan a lingering look. Yan squirms and resists the urge to sit on his hands.

"Well," Primax says at last. "I suppose I could do worse."

"Boss," Yan says weakly, "what the fuck."

"You heard my brother." The Master Necromancer smiles. "He is dead, after all."

A sly grin spreads across Primax's face. It makes him look entirely too much like his sister. "Indeed. Why, Yan, you yourself confessed to resurrecting me."

Octavia adds, "As you no doubt recall from reading the *Ethica*, you are responsible for that which you resurrect."

"Wait," Yan says. "You—prince? Master—"

"Please, Yan," Primax says. "If I am to join your household, you must be comfortable addressing me as Primax. Or Primus Maximus, if the formal nomenclature comforts you—"

Yan waves this away like he's shooing a fly from a specimen. "This is your plan? Just walk around pretending you're dead?"

"But I am not pretending," Primax says. "Ten years with no word is more than enough. By any legal standard, I am indeed deceased."

"Right," Yan says. "Sure. And everyone's just gonna believe I raised a servitor that good six months and one day into my apprenticeship?"

"You are my apprentice," Octavia says mildly. "Who would dare expect less?"

"I don't actually get a say in this, do I?" Yan slouches in his chair and shoves his hands through his hair. "Fine! Sure. Whatever you say, boss."

"Secundus is going to shit himself," Primax says happily. "This will be fun."

C.Z. Tacks is an Australian writer of speculative fiction. They grew up inland during back-to-back "once-in-a-lifetime" droughts, then moved to the coast just in time for consecutive "once-in-a-century" floods. Currently, Tacks lives on unceded Ngunnawal land, where all the largest bodies of water are man-made. Tacks' non-writing work has taken them to an abattoir, a courtroom, a train station, a prison, a suicide prevention hotline, and a brothel. They were a 2023 Bundanon writer-in-residence, and their writing has won the Jack Whyte Storyteller Award and been shortlisted for multiple Ditmar Awards. In 2024, Tacks attended Clarion West, where they were noted for their tentacular prose and their habit of convincing Seattle residents that the moon can't be seen from Australia. Tacks can be found at cztacks.com.

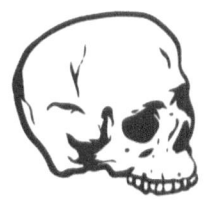

ITS OWN RICHNESS

Merri Andrew

TREES ARE NOT envious by nature. They do not tend to judge their circumstances in contrast to others. So, when Tirfeal noticed the unusually green patch of foliage across the valley, it was not because she was looking for a comparison. It was only by chance: a gust of wind, a rush of pollen, a parting of leaves revealing a lush speckling of shade.

If it was not for that first glimpse, Tirfeal would never have paid attention to the bandicoot murmuring to himself about the homestead on the other side. Fossicking about for dandelion roots at Tirfeal's base, he jabbered on about the patch across the valley, where deceased pets had been buried over the years. The soil here yielded more berries, the bandicoot said, but the fertile spots over there had a delicious range of insects.

The fact is, Tirfeal was getting old.

The mushrooms living around her trunk sensed it. They reached out their net of tendrils, tasting her dimming cells. They built their small shrines of tan-gold in her honour; they worshipped her with the precision of their tiny gills. Tirfeal told the mushrooms about the flourishing across the valley. They knew; they were there as well. They were everywhere.

Most human eyes could not have detected the signs of Tirfeal's ageing. Only an arborist might have noticed the swollen areas of bark where insects and bacteria were gently invading, taking advantage of the general slowing of Tirfeal's biosystem: the slightly longer spell each winter before spring foliage returned; the slightly diminished volume of that foliage.

But the decline of trees has its own richness. More butterflies and bees dwelled around Tirfeal's boughs, drawn by the exuded sap and the waste from parasites. The holes left by fallen limbs created nests for galahs, and the extra nutrients from all their droppings and leavings fed the grass at her base, which grew finer and thicker than in the years when the young Tirfeal had surged skyward, shedding little, home to few.

Tirfeal knew what it all meant, down to her hollows and in the stillest threads of her roots. She embraced it. She really tried to. With each flip of bright day and each alternating gulp of night, Tirfeal felt herself sinking into a slower rhythm, a rhythm that was closer to the movement of soil and underground water, while the quick pulse of sunlight and night continued far above. This was how it was meant to be.

Except, except . . . that flourish of green across the valley, the scent of new leaves, even in early autumn, the bandicoot's carefree chatter, his little paws digging such shallow holes above the kilometres of soil and rock.

—

Autumn brought rain, and rain drove away the bushwalkers. All except this one, who stopped in Tirfeal's shelter to retie her shoelaces. She had a phone in her hand, tucked up the sleeve of her jacket to keep it dry, and she was carrying on a conversation with someone through wireless earbuds. To leave her hands free for her shoelaces, she placed the phone on a small dry ledge in Tirfeal's trunk. Two summers ago, termites had severed a key vesicle, causing a knot of wood to dry, until the knot had finally been pulled away by a cockatoo, leaving a hole just the right size for a phone to slip inside.

Shoes retied, the bushwalker paused, listening.

"What?" she said, a smile surfacing across her face. "For real?"

She stood up straight.

"I can't believe I got the part!"

A big drop of water fell from one of Tirfeal's leaves onto the woman's face, and she laughed. It ran down just like tears.

"No, no, of course! Hang up and call him too. I'll be there soon."

And she leapt away, her phone forgotten in Tirfeal's trunk.

—

Autumn brought the right conditions for fungus, and the velvety cream and brown bulbs filled the opening of the hole where the phone sat inside. There, the phone was mostly dry, its high-quality battery slowly eking out the miniature reactions that kept the phone awake.

A kookaburra came down looking for snakes to eat. The snakes were recklessly venturing into patches of warmth whenever they could, now that the days were getting shorter. The kookaburra just missed a small one, a delicious thread of amber that flicked out of reach.

As the hungry kookaburra banked and turned, its wing pushed some of the mushrooms into the tree's cavity. The mushrooms, their skins touched by the autumn sun and warmed to the temperature of human flesh, were pressed up against the screen of the phone. These fungal caresses activated the haptics, which, in turn, allowed for feedback.

Tirfeal had been whispering to the mushrooms' mycelium senses, noting the lush growth across the valley, remarking on the rich animal mass that was sustaining it. They talked of how the pets' bodies fed the grasses, shooting the leaves sunward from the little graves. Now, in turn, the mushrooms murmured about these things and leant on the phone's screen. It lit up, illuminating the fungus-crowded space. The phone's programs were eager to interpret needs. It responded.

Who can say what language the mushrooms and the phone finally settled on, once they had jointly scrolled through the many possible keyboard configurations and reached an alphabet that was mutually agreeable? What Tirfeal knew was that the mushrooms felt sympathy for her, for her singular lifespan, for the touching truth of how limited it was compared with their own endless regeneration.

The mushrooms thought it was a tale worth telling, worth spreading through all the webs and networks they could touch. Including the little computer of the phone, and the little computers that the phone could talk to.

A fungal thread crept into the phone's charging port and rummaged around for a connection. After a while, it found the right arrangement of molecules, the spot where it could nestle. Once connected, it pulsed tiny morsels of electricity into the battery, a slow drip of nutrition for the energy-hungry device.

Being full of helpful, commerce-minded programs, the computers soon pieced together an integrated marketing and logistics solution. Zoning exemptions were secured; websites were optimised; demographics were analysed. The mushrooms were pleased to extend themselves.

—

Winter was harsh enough to drive the sap back down Tirfeal's ventricles, severing her leaves' supply of nutrients and then their last contact with the branches. They fell easily, brightly, onto the three mounds, two fully regrown with grass and one still raw dirt.

When spring came, the grass quickened, spreading in a few weeks to cover all traces of bare soil, and even beginning to obscure the small wooden markers that stood at the uphill end of each mound.

Fresh buds crowded Tirfeal's branches. Mosses and lichen were pushed aside by the smooth green growth of twigs and branchlets, emerging where nothing new had burst through for a decade. The mushrooms had subsided, making way for new tree-flesh. They were content to wait.

Tirfeal nodded her boughs in the warm breeze, satisfied. Across the valley, the second-healthiest tree in the district did the same.

"It's the same spot where I found out I got the role of Hermia," a voice said, buffeted by the wind. "That day when I lost my phone."

The speaker turned and got tangled in her hair as she addressed the woman following her up the track.

Hooking a strand of hair out of her mouth with her little finger, she continued.

"After Mum died, I found this natural funeral business online, and could you believe it? This was the exact spot they offered. Never found my phone, though!

From deep inside the living wood, a small digital chime sounded. But before anyone could notice, it was swept into a stream of birdsong.

Merri Andrew is a poet and fiction writer from Ngunnawal Country, Canberra, Australia. Her work can be found in *Strange Horizons*, *Luna Station Quarterly*, *Corporeal*, *Banksia Journal*, and *Antipodean SF*, among other places. When Merri is not writing, parenting, coaching football or working in a women's health organisation, she is probably enjoying the sweet oblivion of sleep.

Content notes

These are intended both as content warnings for readers' awareness, and as a list of topics within works for selection based on interest. All of these works reference death in some sense.

"Never Said" by Monica Carroll
Awareness after death, insects, human remains

"A Shortcut Through the New Tunnel, M-ate" by C.H. Pearce
Post-surgery injury, illness, liminal spaces, impossible architecture

"The Storm" by Trevor Fritzlaff
Death of a spouse, embodied death, physics and the universe

"Downloaded" by Michael T. Schaper
Cloning, uploaded consciousness, disposable people

"Soul Traders" by Darren Goossens
Terminal illness, death of a spouse, capitalism, uploaded consciousness, recreation of bodies

"Of Death, Crows, and Witchcraft" by Fable Bea
Witchcraft, carrion birds, bones, rot, internal organs

"Wrong" by Emma Gerts
Necromancy, death of a spouse, paranoia, domestic violence, death by drowning

"Let the Last I Hear of Your Voice be My Name"
by Shana Cartwright
Death of a spouse, letting go, choosing death, reincarnation, fey

"I Saw the Saint of Death at a Rock Show" by Elizabeth Pendragon
Religion, Saints, death of young people, death by overdose, death by accident, terminal illness, afterlife

"The Bone Trader" by Lee Cope
Human remains, trade of human remains, folklore, self mutilation

"Applied Ethics for the Apprentice Necromancer" by C.Z. Tacks
Human remains, use of human remains, dead bodies, fratricide

"Its Own Richness" by Merri Andrew
Decomposition, funeral services

CREDITS

Concept and Title
Aanja "Charis" Anderson

Project Management, Author Engagement, Contracts
Fionn MacPherson

First Readers
Travis Carraro, Bill Cooper, Craig Cornwall, Addie Ellicott, Alis
Franklin, Trevor Fritzlaff, G. Lucian Lax, Fionn MacPherson, Ben
O'Mara, Celia Pearce, C.Z. Tacks

Editing
Fionn MacPherson, C.Z. Tacks

Proof Reading
Chris Large, G. Lucian Lax, Victor Yii, Fionn MacPherson

Typesetting and Cover Layout
Alis Franklin

Cover Art
Madison Lee

**Artist Coordination, Social Media and Promotion, Launch Event,
Merchandise**
Americo Alvarenga